HERO
BY NIGHT

Also by Sara Jane Stone

Caught in the Act
Full Exposure
Command Control
Command Performance

HERO BY NIGHT

BOOK THREE: INDEPENDENCE FALLS

SARA JANE STONE

AVONIMPULSE
An Imprint of HarperCollinsPublishers

This is a work of fiction. Names, characters, places, and incidents are products of the author's imagination or are used fictitiously and are not to be construed as real. Any resemblance to actual events, locales, organizations, or persons, living or dead, is entirely coincidental.

EPub Edition JANUARY 2015 ISBN: 9780062389138

Print Edition ISBN: 9780062389121

10 9 8 7 6 5 4 3 2 1

For Jill (aka the Best Agent Ever), thank you for your awesome advice and insights!

Acknowledgments

I HAVE A long list of people to thank, beginning with my wonderful readers! I deeply appreciate your enthusiasm for this series. Thank you for taking the time to read, review, and chat with me on Facebook! A special shout-out to my Facebook friends who suggested names for the Independence Falls pizza place. I hope you like my final choice! And thank you to everyone who posted pictures of golden retrievers. You helped shape Hero's character!

I am fortunate to have a wonderful and supportive family. My mother and mother-in-law have spent countless hours babysitting while I write. On the weekends when I need to lose myself in the story for twenty-four hours, my husband always offers to take the kids. And without the knowledge of my husband's stepfather and father, this book would not be the same! Thank you to Larry Blair for his insights into the helicopter logging industry. Robert Tormey, you have my heartfelt gratitude for sharing your knowledge about firearms and Oregon shooting ranges. Any mistakes are my own.

Thank you to Jill Marsal at the Marsal Lyon Literary Agency for your continued support. Amanda Bergeron, I feel so blessed to work with such a talented editor. And to everyone at Avon—thank you for your continued support!

While researching this story, I discovered the Women Veterans Interactive, a nonprofit founded to meet all women veterans at their specific points of need. The stories and statistics shared on their site inspired Lena's character. To learn more, please visit womenveteransinteractive.org.

Chapter 1

"THIRTY MINUTES," LENA murmured. "That has to be a record."

Lena Clark stared at the Cascade Mountains, the postcard-perfect backdrop to the backyard barbecue on the verge of turning into a full-blown party. Hero, her golden retriever, sat at her feet by the man-made pond in Eric Moore's yard. Although the cleared field behind the sprawling timber-framed structure, home to the owner of the largest timber operation in Oregon, could hardly be classified as a "yard." Inside the Portland city limits, where she'd lived on and off for the past six years—more off than on, really, due to training and deployments—people had the traditional postage stamp–size grassy areas behind their homes.

But she'd escaped Portland. And landed in Independence Falls, hoping to find her way to normal. Now she was thirty minutes closer.

"I talked to half the people here," Lena continued, her fingers brushing her dog's golden fur. Hero's ears perked up, his head cocked to one side in what she'd come to think of as his I'm-listening expression. A stuffed yellow duck, the doggie toy she'd bought to keep him from chewing on furniture, hung from his mouth. "I mingled without running away and hiding."

She hadn't shaken a single hand, and Hero had been by her side the entire time, but she wasn't looking for major breakthroughs or big victories. At twenty-eight, she knew a war was not won overnight. It took time, bravery, and determination. She possessed all of those things. Even if she had lost more than she liked to admit on the battlefield—like the ability to let anyone get close to her.

"Hey, Lena. Are you OK?"

She turned at the sound of Katie Summers's voice, glancing past her friend to the crowd gathered on the blue stone patio. "Fine. I just needed some space from the party."

And a chance to talk to her dog . . .

OK, so maybe normal was still out of reach.

"Georgia told me that you were looking for a place to stay," Katie said.

"Just for a night, maybe two. I'm planning to find my own apartment soon." Along with a job and her equilibrium. "But I wanted to give Georgia and Eric some space seeing as Nate is visiting his grandmother."

"You think they might get down and dirty on the kitchen table while the three-year-old is out of town?"

"Yes. I do." Lena looked up the hill. Eric stood behind

Georgia, his arms wrapped around her waist, holding her close against his body. Georgia held a beer in one hand, her other reaching back, brushing against Eric's leg as if she had to touch him. The kitchen table would only be the beginning for those two—if their home was free and clear of a guest who moved in for a couple of nights, and more than a week later, still hadn't left.

"The apartment over our barn is yours for as long as you need it," Katie said.

"Your brothers won't mind?" Lena slipped her hands into the hidden pockets in her long halter dress. Katie still lived with her three older brothers on their family farm. Granted, Josh, the youngest of the three, was in the hospital right now recuperating from a logging accident that had landed him in a coma. But Chad and Brody might object to Katie lending out the apartment to an almost-stranger. Lena hadn't met Chad yet, but she knew the family was close and the brothers were protective of their little sister.

Liam Trulane, Georgia's older brother and the man head-over-heels in love with Katie, might not like the idea either. "And you don't need it?"

"Liam and I have other plans," Katie said. "Far away from my brothers' watchful eyes. There is a spare key under a rock to the left of the door. Once you're inside, move it to the right and take the key upstairs with you. That is the in-use signal."

"But Hero—"

Katie's expression turned serious. "Lena, I would never ask you to leave Hero behind. He's welcome in the apartment too."

Lena felt a rush of relief. The thought of leaving her golden retriever outside, even for a night, sent her barreling toward panic. "Thank you."

"You're welcome. Maybe I'll see you tomorrow? Georgia and I were planning to take a hike. Nothing crazy. I made her promise."

"Sure." Lena knew all about Georgia's need for adventure, the drive that had followed Georgia home from a war zone. And Lena understood it too. Probably more than most, even if she didn't share the same pull. PTSD refused to follow a linear, predetermined path. Nightmares and survivor's guilt haunted Georgia. Those symptoms were on Lena's list, but anxiety topped the chart.

In Lena's shattered world, every little touch triggered fear. If her ex or one of her friends wrapped an arm around her, took her hand, or pulled her into a hug, she would brace for an attack. Fear would build until panic won. And afterward, once it receded, she'd sink further into depression, cutting herself off from the world around her.

Anxiety had become her constant companion, leading her to an isolated place. Until she'd decided to do something about it, entering therapy and finding the golden retriever lying at her feet, gnawing on a stuffed dog toy.

Katie turned to head up the hill. Lena watched, wondering if she should go back to the party and try for another thirty minutes. She scanned the group of people mingling and drinking—and spotted him.

Jeans and a button-down flannel shirt hugged his body, not too tight, but enough to suggest that this man had muscles begging to be touched. He raised a hand, running it through his short, wavy brown hair. Everything about him screamed for hands-on exploration. That chiseled jaw, the light dusting of stubble as if he hadn't shaved in a day, the way he smiled . . .

Lena drew a sharp breath and tried to look away. But her brain short-circuited and her eyes refused. His sex appeal flowed down the grassy slope like rushing water. And if she weren't careful it would sweep her off her feet, and leave her fighting for air. Looking at him, she wished the road to normal led straight to orgasms.

He turned his head and their gazes met across the empty space. And she swore his warm, I-promise-you'll-like-me-if-you-get-to-know-me grin touched his eyes.

Lena dropped her gaze to the ground, breaking the contact. He wasn't touching her, not even close. But that smile . . .

She turned to face the water. It was better not to look at what she couldn't have. And that man—he was one giant step beyond thirty minutes of small talk.

Sometimes beauty knocked a man on his ass, leaving him damn near desperate for a taste, a touch, and hopefully a round or two between the sheets—or tied up in them. The knockout blonde with the large golden retriever at her feet took the word "beautiful" to a new level.

Chad Summers stared at her, unable to look away or dim the smile on his face. He usually masked his interest better, stopping short of looking like he was begging for it before learning a woman's name. But this mysterious beauty had special written all over her.

She stared at him, her gaze open and wanting. For a heartbeat. Then she turned away, her back to the party as she stared out at Eric Moore's pond.

Her hair flowed in long waves down her back. One look left him wishing he could wrap his hand around her shiny locks and pull. His gaze traveled over her back, taking in the outline of gentle curves beneath her flowing, and oh-so-feminine, floor-length dress. Chad had nothing against jeans on a woman. But he loved clothes that offered access to a woman's legs. The thought of the beauty's long skirt decorating her waist propelled him into motion. Chad headed in her direction, moving away from the easy, quiet conversation about God-knew-what on the patio.

He appreciated the fact that Eric Moore—who'd recently become his boss/business partner after Moore Timber bought the Summers Family Trucking business—had decided to throw a party celebrating Chad's little brother's return to the land of awake and alert. But the laid-back gathering lacked excitement. Music. Dancing. Something more than a small group of people he'd known most of his life—three dozen at most—drinking beers and eating burgers.

The blonde, a mysterious stranger in a sea of familiar faces, might be the spark this party needed. He was a few feet away when the dog abandoned his post at her side and cut Chad off. Either the golden retriever was protecting his owner, or the animal was in cahoots with the familiar voice calling his name.

"Chad Summers!"

The blonde turned at the sound, looking first at him,

her blue eyes widening as if surprised at how close he stood, and then at her dog. From the other direction, a familiar face with short black hair—Susan maybe?—marched toward him.

Without a word, Maybe Susan stopped by his side and raised her glass. With a dog in front of him, trees to one side, and an angry woman on his other, there was no escape.

"Hi there." He left off her name just in case he'd guessed wrong, but offered a warm, inviting smile. Most women fell for that grin, but if Maybe Susan had at one time—and seeing her up close, she looked very familiar, though he could swear he'd never slept with her—she wasn't falling for it today.

She poured the cool beer over his head, her mouth set in a firm line. "That was for my sister. Susan Lewis? You spent the night with her six months ago and never called."

Chad nodded, silently grateful he hadn't addressed the pissed-off woman by her sister's name. "My apologies, ma'am."

"You're a dog," Susan's sister announced. The animal at his feet stepped forward as if affronted by the comparison.

"For the past six months, my little sister has talked about you, saving every article about your family's company," the angry woman continued.

Whoa . . . Yes, he'd taken Susan Lewis out once and they'd ended the night back at his place, but he could have sworn they were on the same page. Hell, he'd heard her say the words, *I'm not looking for anything serious*, and he'd believed her. It was one freaking night. He didn't think he needed signed documents that spelled out his intentions and hers.

"She's practically built a shrine to you," she added, waving her empty beer cup. "Susan was ready to plan your wedding."

"Again, I'm sorry, but it sounds like there was a miscommunication." Chad withdrew a bandana from his back pocket, one that had belonged to his father, and wiped his brow. "But wedding bells are not in my future. At least not anytime soon."

The angry sister shook her head, spun on her heels, and marched off.

Chad turned to the blonde and offered a grin. She looked curious, but not ready to run for the hills. "I guess I made one helluva first impression."

"Hmm." She glanced down at her dog as if seeking comfort in the fact that he stood between them.

"I'm Chad Summers." He held out his hand—the one part of his body not covered in beer.

"You're Katie's brother." She glanced briefly at his extended hand, but didn't take it.

He lowered his arm, still smiling. "Guilty."

"Lena." She nodded to the dog. "That's Hero."

"Nice to meet you both." He looked up the hill. Country music drifted down from the house. Someone had finally added some life to the party. Couples moved to the beat on the blue stone patio, laughing and drinking under the clear Oregon night sky. In the corner, Liam Trulane tossed logs into a fire pit.

"After I dry off," Chad said, turning back to the blonde, "how about a dance?"

"No."

Chad waited for an excuse, expecting a lie—her dog would be lonely or she had a boyfriend. That latter one, lie or not, would send him on his way. But she didn't say another word.

He stepped toward her, as close as the dog would allow. He was close enough to smell her floral scent. It was too faint for a perfume, most likely her soap. There was a hint of lavender and a touch of honey. As if the sight of her wasn't enough, the smell made him want to taste her. He leaned in, a fraction of an inch, nothing more. But the next thing he knew, her dog was pushing at his legs.

"Hero is protective of my space." Lena's voice had a breathless quality that suggested maybe this time she wished her dog would butt out. Or maybe that was his imagination.

Chad moved back, looking at the golden retriever with renewed interest. For a breed with a reputation for being kind and friendly, this one looked as if he was debating dropping his chew toy and sinking his teeth into Chad's leg.

"So what brings you two to Independence Falls?" he asked, keeping one eye on Hero.

"Georgia offered me a place to stay. While I get back on my feet."

"Between jobs?" The rest of the country might be headed toward recovery, but rural Oregon was still suffering high unemployment. A lot of people around here were doing their best to "get back on their feet."

"I guess you could say that," she said.

She didn't give an inch. And hell, he liked that. Rocking back on his heels, Chad pretended to think. "What did you do before? I might know someone who is looking."

"It doesn't matter," she said. "I can't go back to it."

"Being a model is that tough?" He offered her a teasing look that he knew for a fact helped separate women from their panties.

Lena raised an eyebrow. "I wouldn't know. And you can drop the sweet-talking act."

"You'd prefer I talk dirty?" Chad cocked his head, studying her. There it was. A spark of interest in her blue eyes. But she hid it quickly.

"I've spent most of my life on army bases. I'm betting you don't have anything I haven't heard before."

So the drop-dead gorgeous, not-a-model woman was a military brat? He took that tidbit and filed it away. He wanted to know more about her—where she'd grown up, where she'd worked, if she screamed during sex or maintained the calm control he was finding wildly attractive.

"I might use some of the same words," he said. "But they would have a different effect on you."

"You're that good with your words?"

"Yes. And that's not the only thing I'm good with." He paused for a beat, expecting a laugh and hoping for a breathy sigh. Nothing. Her face was an impartial mask. "So how about that dance? I could whisper naughty things in your ear."

"No." The way she said that one word sounded like a reflex.

"A walk under the stars?"

"Romantic, but I can't." She stepped away even though he'd been careful not to move a muscle in her direction. "I wish I could."

This time her words were not a quick dismissal. She said the word "wish" with the fervor of a kid looking up to the stars and asking for a snow day in July. Hell, if there was one thing he understood, it was wishing and hoping for things he couldn't have.

His mother walking through the front door to the farmhouse and admitting that leaving her family had been a mistake . . . His dad seated beside him in a helicopter one last time. . .

"Can I ask you something?" Chad said.

She nodded. A strand of blond hair fell across her face and he resisted the urge to brush it away. With any other woman, he would not have thought twice about an innocent touch in a public space. But he sensed Lena had boundaries that demanded respect.

"Where did you meet Georgia?"

"In therapy."

The words, coupled with her matter-of-fact tone, nearly knocked him on his ass. "You're a veteran. I never would have guessed that one."

"A little different from a model," she said with a small smile. "I was in the army. Until eighteen months ago."

"The job you can't go back to," he said, shifting his weight from one foot to the other.

She nodded, her blue eyes trained on him as if tracking

his movements. Had someone hurt her? The thought of it pissed him off. Or had the time spent serving her country left her battle-scarred on the inside? Either way, he wasn't the man to fix her problems. He'd never been drawn to wounded creatures.

Chad glanced at the dog. Whatever had happened to her, Lena already had her hero. She didn't need him. And he didn't want a woman in his life he couldn't walk away from come sunrise. Or a woman he couldn't touch . . .

He looked up at the patio and spotted another blonde. With her jeans and low-cut blouse, the other woman possessed the same petite build as Lena. But there was nothing striking about her. Looking at her didn't leave him wanting to pull her hair, or hear his name on her lips, never mind learn her secrets.

"She looks like fun," Lena said.

Busted.

He glanced at the woman who made him want to do all those things and more. "Sure you're not?"

"I can be," she said with a wry smile, as if this bit of information was a carefully guarded secret. "But not the kind you're in the market for. Not tonight."

"That's a shame. I was looking forward to whispering dirty things in your ear."

She pursed her lips, her eyes filled with wistful wanting. "I'm not ready for that kind of fun," she said, her voice low, but certain. "Not yet."

"That's fair." Yeah, those words made it crystal clear she wasn't up for his no-strings-attached, down-and-dirty nights. But it didn't keep him from hoping.

"If that changes, I'd like to know," he added. Chad slowly backed away from the woman and her dog, offering her one last smile. "Try and have a good time tonight, Lena. This is a party."

"I'll take that under consideration," she said, the golden retriever returning to her side. "Good-bye, Chad Summers."

Chapter 2

CHAD STARED AT the naked woman on the bed and wondered if he was making a mistake. Lying on her stomach, with her face buried in the pillow, Amber's long blond hair fell in a dozen different directions—straight up, over the pillow, and down the smooth slope of her bare-naked back. His gaze drifted lower. A thin white sheet covered her ass, but he could see enough to guess she'd abandoned her underwear. Given how hot it was in the cramped studio apartment, he was ready to shed his clothes too. The heat was on despite the fact that it was unseasonably warm for fall in Oregon. He could hear the water rattling through the radiators. And she hadn't bothered to turn on the fan before passing out.

He moved to the kitchenette counter and switched on the small desktop fan. It wasn't much, but it would feel good when they got hot and sweaty. The blades rotated, blowing the sheet off her body.

His mouth fell open as he drank in the view. From where he was standing, waking up sleeping beauty no longer seemed like a mistake.

How had she hidden those curves earlier? When they'd talked and danced at the party, he'd never suspected her waist curved in such a way that it begged to be touched. Or that her low back led to an ass that would put most swimsuit models to shame.

Chad unbuttoned his shirt, stripped it off, and tossed it aside. Stepping closer, he debated how to wake her. Call her name? Or climb in bed beside her and wait until she felt him?

When he'd given Amber instructions on how to find the hidden key to the guest apartment over the barn, he'd expected to find her awake and eager to do all the naughty things she'd whispered in his ear at Eric Moore's cookout. The bubbly blonde had made it clear she wanted him for one night—nothing more—before she returned to California.

But then Amber had left the party to stop by her cousin's house and pick up a few things while he'd rushed home for a quick shower to rinse off the beer.

Chad shook his head, still stunned he'd had a beer dumped on him in the middle of a party. Maybe he deserved it for not calling Susan back. But he'd never made her any promises. He didn't have to remember Susan to know that. He never made anyone promises beyond the here and now. And it sucked that Susan's sister decided to seek revenge in front of Lena.

Lena. Hell. Chad closed his eyes, his hands frozen

on the waistband on his jeans. If he was being honest, he didn't want the passed-out, gorgeous, and eager-to-rock-his-world woman in his bed. He wanted Lena. With her blond hair, blue eyes, and perfect heart-shaped face, Lena looked as if she'd walked out of a Greek myth. Chad didn't remember much from that class, but the story about the girl who launched a thousand ships stuck with him. Lena possessed the kind of beauty that would start battles, but instead she'd fought in them. And if the golden retriever that followed her around offered any indication, she'd come back with some serious baggage.

As a rule, he steered clear of women with issues. He liked a good time, plain and simple. Nothing that could tie him down, or bind him to a person who might walk away without a backward glance. He'd been through that once, watching the door slam behind his mother. As a kid, Chad had witnessed his father's heartbreak. And he wasn't eager to follow him down that path.

But with Lena, he felt a connection.

"Fuck me, I sound like a freaking girl," Chad murmured, opening his eyes as he unbuttoned his jeans. "Worrying about connections."

The woman on the bed moved as his if roused by his words. Without turning over, she stretched her arms overhead and pressed her palms against the wooden headboard. Her back arched, lifting her hips in the air, her breasts resting against the sheets.

His mouth went dry. The things he could do to her in that position. His hands on her hips, pushing into her . . .

Or if she rolled over, his mouth on her, tasting every inch of her.

"That's it, baby," he said, his voice low. Without taking his eyes off her, he removed his pants and boxers. "Spread your legs for me. Let me see you."

She obeyed, offering a glimpse at the one part of her body he planned to worship until the sun rose. And then she lowered back down, rocking her hips against the mattress. He swore he heard a moan.

"Just wait until I touch you." His voice was a rough growl that spoke volumes about how much he freaking loved the way she responded to his words. "I want to find your sweet spots, running my hands over your shoulders, down your back to your perfect ass. I'm going to explore every wet and wanting inch of you. Taste you. Make you scream. And I'll make damn sure you're with me, begging for more every step of the way."

He heard a soft gasp and his gaze snapped to her head, watching as she rolled over. She kept her arms stretched above her head. The pillow shifted, but not enough to catch a glimpse at her face. Her back arched again, this time thrusting her breasts up, inviting him to tease her nipples . . . And yeah, he wasn't trying to see her pretty eyes anymore.

To hell with holding back. Maybe this blond beauty wouldn't start a war. But the sight of her on his bed, her long legs rubbing together as if seeking something to soothe the ache, dismissed his reservations. Common sense took a backseat to the need radiating from his lower half.

Chad knelt on the bed, half expecting her to toss aside the pillow and reach for him. The woman he'd met earlier, who'd teased him about bathing in beer hops as she'd moved closer, using every excuse to touch him—he'd expected her to be straightforward in the bedroom. The way Amber was moving, responding to his words without giving up the pretense of sleep, didn't seem like her type of game. But then maybe she was still asleep.

Chad frowned. No fucking way.

"I'm going to touch you now," he said, just in case she bolted upright when he reached for her.

A muffled moan was his only response, but it was something.

"Starting at your collarbone," he continued, his finger running the length of the curved bone from shoulder to neck. Keeping his touch featherlight, he followed her sternum down to the valley between her breasts. His thumb brushed the side. "Baby, I swear, I could spend all night, right here, worshipping your breasts."

Maybe his mind was playing tricks on him, but he swore he saw her nipples tighten further. Earlier, he'd been pretty damn sure she was wearing one of those fancy push-up bras that made for mouth-watering cleavage, but often left him with a weird feeling that a bait and switch had taken place when the clothes hit the floor. He had nothing against small breasts, like the ones currently begging for his touch. Hell, he often preferred them, loving the way they responded to teasing.

He bent over, unable to resist a taste. His lips wrapped around her nipple as his tongue flicked back and forth.

Oh hell yes, her breasts proved his theory. Smaller meant more sensitive. And if that wasn't a scientific truth, well, he didn't give a damn. Right now, the woman writhing beneath him, lacing her fingers through his hair as if determined to see if he'd meant what he said when he swore he could spend the night right here, tasting her, was his sole focus.

But he wanted so much more than a taste. Running his teeth over her sensitive flesh, he released her right breast and headed for the left, shifting his legs, positioning one on either side of her. Hovering above her, his body begged for more. He lowered down, letting her feel how she turned him on, his cock pressing against her thigh.

"I fucking *want* you," he murmured, his lips never losing touch with her skin. "All of you. I want your legs wrapped around me, heels digging in, asking for more. I want you on your stomach, your ass in the air, my hand wrapped in your hair. I want to pull back and see your face, watch you come. I want to learn what makes you scream, what turns you on."

Reality and consciousness threatened, but Lena fought them, clinging to sleep. She'd spent the past year dreaming in vivid color. Some nights, when she closed her eyes, surprisingly real soundscapes and horrific sights haunted her. Images of men lying on the ground, their blood flowing over the dirt, their eyes vacant, or worse, pleading for a miracle, filled her nightmares. For some, she'd delivered that miracle, carrying them to safety while bullets sped past her. But knowing they'd lived didn't change the fact that she usually woke up in a panic, as if she'd been in hand-to-hand combat with her memories.

Still, she hadn't had a nightmare in months. They'd faded over time. But she never would have guessed that when the dreams returned, they would include the deep rumble of a man's voice talking dirty to her, or the surprisingly real sensations radiating from her breasts.

The sleeping pill. She hadn't taken one in six months. Not since she'd gotten her dog. But tonight she'd decided to keep Hero in the bathroom, knowing he'd try to sleep on the bed beside her. And this was not her bed. Not everyone appreciated golden retriever hair covering everything—or chew marks on their furniture. Hero was a well-trained service dog in some respects, but he still enjoyed a good chair leg when no one was looking.

So she'd taken half a pill hoping to black out, or dream of unicorns frolicking under rainbows, not have an orgasm.

The feeling of a warm mouth against her chest vanished.

No, she wasn't complaining! This was by far the Best. Dream. Ever.

"Don't stop," she whispered. "I haven't felt like this in so long. So good. So . . ."

Close to normal.

"Just good?" the sexy voice murmured. "Beautiful, I can do better than good."

"How?" Her voice was faint and she doubted he'd heard her.

Skilled hands moved over her breasts, teasing her nipples with a potent combination of pressure and featherlight touches. Her hands fell back to the bed, clutching the sheets, as a warm mouth kissed her neck.

"If you liked my mouth on your breasts," he said, his lips still touching her skin, "imagine how you'll feel when I move between your legs, spread your thighs wide, and taste you." His tongue flicked back and forth against her neck. Once. Twice. A potent demonstration of what he wanted to do to her. "I'll drive you wild."

"Promise?" she gasped.

His teeth nipped at her neck. "Yes."

"Oh." It wasn't a word. It was a moan.

He lowered his hips, grinding nine, maybe more, hard inches against her. Not rough, but in a way that made her crave him. He felt big and thick pressed against her. But this was her dream. Why settle for average, when you could conjure up a man with a dirty mouth and an erection guaranteed to get the job done? She had a greater chance of seeing a unicorn walking down the street than actually going to bed with a man like this. If this were real, she'd be terrified right now. Intimate contact . . . she wasn't there yet.

His lips brushed her jaw. She felt cool air on her face. She'd lost her pillow. Her fingers dug into the sheets, clutching them hard, the pleasure waning now. Warning bells rang out in her mind.

Oh no, this was not what the beginning of an orgasm felt like.

Lips—real, warm, demanding lips—kissed hers, and it felt as if the blood running through her veins turned to ice. Her heart raced and her breaths came in short, desperate gasps. She fought for oxygen. It was as if someone had strapped her into a car, taped her foot to the gas, and taken away the brakes. The fear mounted. If she didn't do something soon, she'd crash.

Lena opened her eyes, forcing her mind and body to push aside the effects of the sleeping pill, and focus. There was a naked man on her. Kissing her. Touching her. This wasn't a dream.

No, it wasn't possible. No one got this close. Not to her.

Instinct took over. She released the sheets and pushed hard against his chest. "Get off me!"

Lightning-fast, he backed away. "What the hell? What's wrong?"

She rolled to her side, reaching for the nightstand drawer, and her Smith & Wesson revolver. She heard a banging against the bathroom door. Her four-legged Hero was coming for her. The lock gave, door swinging open as her retriever rushed out his teeth bared.

She felt the bed shift as the man who had kissed her moved away. Gun in hand, she rolled onto her back and focused on her target, struggling to get her ragged breathing under control.

"Chad? Chad Summers?" She blinked, starring at the man who had flirted with her, teasing her by Eric Moore's pond. The man she'd *wanted.*

He held his hands up, palms out in a show of surrender,

his gaze moving back and forth between the revolver in her hands and the growling golden retriever, who looked ready and willing to sink his canine teeth into the part of Chad Summers's body she'd felt pressed up against her.

"Lena," he said evenly. "I can explain. But first, I need you to put the gun down and call off your dog."

Chapter 3

THERE WAS NO question that tonight was one giant mistake. But unlike most errors in judgment, this one had resulted in a meet and greet with a gun and a dog that wanted to play fetch with his balls.

Chad studied Lena, waiting for her to lower her weapon as the dog growled at his feet. His desire had dried up the minute she'd said, "Get off." He didn't need a gun waved in his face to prove her point. But he sure as hell wanted a chance to explain before he hightailed it out the door. "Lena, I need you to lower your weapon."

"You kissed me."

"Yes." He'd done a lot more, but he had a feeling pointing that out would not help reunite the gun with the nightstand. "And was it so bad that you want to shoot me?"

Who the hell gave a loaded weapon to the woman who needed a dog at her side to get through the freaking day?

"I'm sorry." She lowered the gun, placing it back in the drawer. "Hero, come here."

"Thank you," he said, reaching for his clothes as soon as the dog joined his owner on the bed. Out of the corner of his eye, he saw her pull the sheet over her naked body. Once he had his boxers and jeans on, he turned to her. "And for the record, I'm sorry too. What happened tonight . . . Hell, I wasn't expecting to find you here."

Lena nodded. "The blonde from the party?"

"Yeah." He retrieved his shirt and pulled it on, making quick work of the buttons. "Amber."

As if saying her name cast a spell bringing her here, a knock sounded on the door at the bottom of the stairs that connected the studio apartment to the outside world. "That's her now."

He headed for the door, needing to stop Amber before they added a witness to their fucked-up little party. "I'll send her home and then we'll talk."

He heard a soft "OK" from the bed and was tempted to glance over his shoulder to see if Lena was in tears. Not much could make this situation worse. But a crying woman? Yeah, that would do it.

"Just think," he muttered, descending the stairs two at a time. "It could be Brody or, shit, Katie at the door. That would be worse."

But he knew where his siblings were tonight. His little sister was doing God knew what with Liam Trulane. OK, maybe Chad had a good idea what they were doing, but he hated thinking about his kid sister doing those things. Brody was at the hospital visiting their youngest brother.

And Chad was the one who'd ended up in bed with a woman who slept with a gun on the nightstand. Too bad Lena was also the woman who took his breath away, she was so damn beautiful. But if he acted on that desire again, shit, she'd find another way to steal his breath.

Chad shook his head as he reached the door and spotted the bubbly Amber on the other side.

FIVE MINUTES LATER, he climbed up the stairs and found Lena sitting on the edge of the queen-size bed wearing the same flowing, floor-length dress she'd had on at the party. The one that probably had beer stains on some of the flowers from when Susan's sister had dumped her drink over Chad's head. Yeah, tonight Lena was seeing him at his best.

"Amber went back to her cousin's house," he said, taking a chair from the small, circular table by the kitchenette and turning it around so the back faced her. He sat down, looking straight at her. "I didn't mention your name. Just told her I was too tired."

"I'm sorry about earlier," Lena said, her voice strong and unwavering, no sign of tears. "Katie told me where to find the key and said I could stay here for tonight."

"Yeah, she kind of forgot to mention that to me."

"It was only for one night. I wanted to give Eric and Georgia some space after the party."

Chad nodded, the pieces of tonight's puzzle falling

into place. But some things didn't add up. "Do you always lock your dog up at night?"

"No." She ran her hand over the golden retriever's head, scratching behind the ears. The big dog leaned closer, begging for more, without ever taking his dark eyes off Chad. "He sleeps with me most nights. In case I need him."

Need him? How many guys climbed into her bed? Sure, she looked like a supermodel, but still, shit like this didn't happen every day.

"I have nightmares sometimes," she added. "Hero helps. But he's sort of an unofficial service dog. He's been trained, but not by one of the sanctioned programs. The waitlist for those programs ranges from one to two years. I didn't think I could wait that long. Hero came from a young trainer, just starting out. He's a great service dog. But he still chews. And sheds. So I put him in the bathroom for the night and took a sleeping pill."

Chad stared at the woman who'd attached a bomb to her matter-of-fact account of her dog's training. A sleeping pill? His stomach flipped and for the first time that night, he thought he might be sick. The pill explained why she'd played along. She'd been ready and willing to make love to a drug-inspired mirage. But it didn't change the fact that he'd climbed into bed with a scared, drugged woman—the one woman in Independence Falls he freaking knew better than to touch.

Lena pressed her fingers into Hero's smooth coat. The horror on Chad's face left her wishing she could walk out of this apartment and away from this night. But she had no place else to go. A hotel maybe, but her bank account was low, and she'd maxed out her last credit card buying dog food.

And she'd been trained from a young age to face her fears head-on. *What doesn't kill you makes you stronger.* Her father's words, not hers.

Every time those words ran through her head, she wondered if the fear she lived with day after day was slowly draining her life. Loud noises and people moving toward her, from any direction, shook her to her core. A simple hug led to panic. She was alive and safe in Oregon. Logically she knew that. The patch of disturbed dirt on the side of the road was not a bomb. But still, she didn't feel strong. She hadn't for the past eighteen months. Until she'd moved to Independence Falls, planning to stay with Georgia, the wild, determined woman from her therapy group, Lena had felt like she was losing the battle.

But Georgia was living proof that a person could be broken and strong at the same time. Lena clung to the hope that here, in this town, she could build a normal life too.

Until Chad Summers climbed into her bed and cracked her hope.

"I thought . . . I thought it was all a dream," she said. "Until you kissed me."

"Lena, I am so sorry. You have no idea—"

"It was an honest mistake," she said quickly. She couldn't handle long, drawn-out apologies. "I'd appreciate if we kept this between us. I like it here. I was hoping for a fresh start in this town."

"I won't say a word." He looked away. "But I can't speak for Amber. I don't know her well."

Lena raised an eyebrow. He didn't know the other woman, but he'd been ready and willing to do all the naughty things he'd spelled out to her—touch her, taste her—with Amber?

"If she says something to Katie, my sister might put two and two together," he continued. "Might be best to head that off and explain I came up here, surprised you, and left. Leave out the naked part."

"That makes sense." Lena nodded, pushing off the bed, dragging the sheet with her. "Let me get my stuff and I'll get out of here."

"Lena, wait." Chad stood too, taking a step forward, reaching for her arm, but then thinking better of it. Or maybe she'd flinched. She'd been working hard to control that reaction, but tonight had thrown her, leaving her troubled mind wondering if every moment was a threat. "You don't have to leave."

"I don't want to be in the way," she said.

He placed his hands on his hips. "It's the middle of the night. Do you have someplace to go?"

"No." The place she'd called home was no longer hers. She'd given it to her ex-husband as part of their divorce six months ago. Right now, she owned a duffel bag filled with clothes and necessities; her revolver; a ten-pound bag of dog food; a giant, always-hungry golden retriever; and a beat-up blue Toyota pickup. "No, I don't."

At twenty-eight, she was a homeless veteran. And she'd drawn a gun on the first man to touch her in months.

What doesn't kill you makes you stronger.

But her father had forgotten to warn her about the humiliation. And that just might slay her.

"Stay. Please," Chad said. "I've made a lot of mistakes tonight. Let me do something right."

"I don't know." She'd never get to sleep now.

"My sister will kill me if she finds out that I chased you out of here."

"Fine. I'll stay." She couldn't afford to make waves, not if she planned to live in Independence Falls. And she didn't want to give Katie Summers a reason to talk.

"Good." Chad smiled. Not the devil-may-care look he'd wielded at the party earlier, the one that had drawn her in and left her wishing she could invite a man like him back to her bed, but a genuine smile. "And Lena, promise me one thing."

"What?"

"Let Hero sleep out here with you. I don't care if he chews the furniture. I want you to feel safe. Promise?"

"Yes." The way he looked at her as if she was too delicate to touch, the way he moved around the room, careful to keep his distance—she might as well have a neon sign about her head flashing "Broken. Stand Back." Part of her wanted to be more like the woman he'd planned to meet in this room. Carefree. Fun. The kind of woman who would melt into his kisses. Instead she was the one who agreed to let her dog sleep next to her even if he chewed up the place.

"I promise," she added.

"Good." He headed for the stairs. "I'll see you around, Lena."

Lena gave a quick nod, even though he wasn't looking at her anymore. She closed her eyes and made a silent promise. She would find the road map to normal and follow it to the end. She'd do anything to get to there. Anything.

Chapter 4

"WE HAVE A problem."

Chad uncrossed his legs and sat up straight in the chair. No one wanted to hear those words from his boss/business partner's mouth at an impromptu Saturday meeting. His mind jumped to last night. Had Eric found out about the misunderstanding with Lena? Shit, if Eric knew he'd probably found out from Georgia, which meant Chad's little sister also knew by now.

The fact that Chad hadn't been the one to tell Katie would count against him. He should have called his sister first thing this morning. But he didn't want to make a big deal about it. And picking up the phone at dawn felt like the act of a guilty man.

"Something I can help with?" Chad asked, going with innocent-until-proven-guilty.

"Yeah." Eric leaned back in his chair. "Your dating life has become a problem."

"Look, if this is about last night, when Susan's sister dumped her drink on me," Chad said, "I swear, I thought we were on the same page. I had no idea Susan had gone and built a freaking shrine."

"This isn't about Susan. Not exactly," Eric said with a sigh. "The pilot who moved here last month from California, the one who flew helicopters for a timber operation down there, one of the only people in the Willamette Valley qualified for the job—"

"I didn't take him out," Chad said, trying for funny even though he didn't feel like laughing. This conversation was headed for a crash and burn. And was driving home the fact that Eric Moore was more boss than business partner. Sure, Chad had contributed to the cost of the helicopter and his name was on the deed, but Moore Timber was still Eric's baby.

"I was planning to grab a beer with the guy to get to know him before we started flying together," Chad added. "But I never asked."

"Too late now. He turned down the chance to be your copilot." Eric ran his hands through his short hair. "He called and left a message this morning. Something about his cousin Amber and last night? He said she came home in tears."

With each word, Chad felt his dreams for the future entering a downward spiral. He opened his mouth to tell Eric about last night. He'd sent Amber home. He hadn't touched her. Because of Lena . . .

Chad pressed his lips together, shaking his head. He couldn't mention Lena and last night to Eric.

"You need a full-time copilot, someone you can work with as part of team."

"This isn't *Top Gun*," Chad said, leaning back in his chair, folding his arms across his chest. "We just need to fly the damn helicopter together."

Eric's mouth formed a grim line. "You need to work together. One guy spotting, making sure you don't hit anything or anyone, and the other keeping the bird in the air. I need to know you won't get into a fight while flying over my harvest site, and my crew for that matter, about who was in your bed the night before. I can't send you up in the air if you're a liability. If we have another helicopter accident, we're screwed and you know it."

Chad nodded, letting out the breath he'd been holding. Yeah, he knew it. And he sure as shit didn't want another family to go through what his had suffered these past few weeks. Chad had witnessed firsthand the damage one of the hooks used to secure the logs to the helicopter could do. His little brother was still in the hospital, his short-term memory a scrambled mess, thanks to a hook to the back of the head.

"Josh's accident happened at the hands of an independent contractor," Eric added. "They'll take the insurance hit and pay the damages. But this is about more than money. It's about the people. I value every member of our crew. I also value our company's position in this community."

"I get it, Eric. Trust me, I spent days sitting by Josh's hospital bed waiting for him to wake up. And he still has a long road ahead of him."

"Good. Then you'll understand why I need to say this. If you want to be a part of Moore Timber, if you want to run the helicopter logging side of this operation, hell, if you want the chance to get up in the air with a copilot at your side, you have to settle down."

Chad's jaw tightened and he felt knots forming in his shoulders. If he wanted to fly for Moore Timber? It was his fucking dream job. He'd grown up flying helicopters with his dad over logging country just for fun on a Saturday afternoon. "I want to work here and fly. You know I do. But you need to spell out what the hell you're asking for, Eric."

"I'm not saying you need to get married." The man across the desk pinched his nose. At moments like this it was easy to forget they were the same age. He'd grown up with Eric, played ball with him. But Chad hadn't turned his family business into the largest timber operation in the Pacific Northwest. Eric had. "But would it kill you to stay with one woman for a while?"

Kill him? No. But as far as he could see, relationships led to heartbreak. His father had crumbled when his mother left. Some things stayed with a kid a helluva lot longer than they should.

Chad pushed to his feet. "You have my word I'll steer clear of the Moore Timber staff and their sisters."

Eric shook his head. "The whole damn town is connected to this place."

"If you're suggesting I need to start something just to keep my job . . . Shit, Eric, I will not lead a woman on, pretending that the thing between us will lead somewhere. I'm honest, man. Always."

"I'm not suggesting you lie, just try to see if one night could become more," Eric said. "Moore Timber is too important. I can't risk losing clients and staff over hurt feelings. Take yourself off the market for a while. But do something."

"Now you're telling me I can't get laid?"

Eric looked him straight in the eye. "Not if it interferes with my business."

As a rule, Lena wore long, flowing dresses. She loved the feel and freedom of fabric billowing around her. But for hiking, she'd chosen cargo shorts, a lightweight long-sleeve shirt, and boots, which felt heavy on her feet as she followed Georgia and Katie up the dirt path to the waterfalls.

"It will be worth it when we get there," Georgia called over her shoulder.

Georgia had spent her days hiking through the Afghan countryside carrying her gear not long ago. Lena had been there too, possibly covering some of the same ground. She wasn't sure, given they'd never talked specifics about their missions. And they probably never would.

Georgia was moving on, barreling toward normal like a tiger charging her prey. Next to her, Lena felt like an inchworm. Lena was doing her best to stay one step ahead of disaster. But that could change at any moment.

Hero brushed against her leg, his tongue hanging out as he panted his way up the path.

"You look about as out of shape as I feel," she murmured. While there was a chance she'd covered the same ground as Georgia, Lena had been out of the army for nearly a year and a half now. And she'd spent most of those early months after she'd returned to the States in her house, paralyzed by fear.

"Water break," Katie called, stopping ten paces ahead of her.

Georgia retraced her steps, pulling out three bottles. "I brought extra if Hero wants some."

"Thanks." Lena took a long drink and focused on reclaiming her breath. Feeling better, she poured water into the small bowl she'd brought for Hero.

"Did the apartment over the barn work out for you?" Katie asked, returning her water bottle to her daypack.

"Yes, but . . . have you talked to Chad today?"

"My brother?" Katie laughed. "He's probably still in bed with the woman he met at the party. I didn't catch her name, but she looked ready and willing to keep him up most of the night. I just hope her cousin isn't the type to defend her misplaced honor when Chad moves on."

"No," Lena said. "He's not."

Katie's brow furrowed. "You know her cousin?"

"Chad is not with Amber. He planned to use the apartment too. He had his own key," Lena explained. "And, well, we ran into each other."

"Oh my God, Lena, I am so sorry," Katie said. "I should have known he'd make a copy and ignore the stupid signal even though he was the one to create it. Did he . . . did he frighten you?"

Yes, but I drew a gun on him would only lead to more questions.

"A little, but he was . . . a perfect gentleman."

Katie snorted. "Chad?"

"Nothing happened," Lena assured her. "He made sure I felt safe, insisted that I stay, and then he left."

"OK. Good." Katie stared at her, long and hard, as if trying to determine if she was telling the truth. "That's good."

Lena picked up Hero's bowl, hoping the conversation would end there. "How much further to the falls?"

"Another mile," Georgia said. "Are you sure you're up for it?"

Lena nodded and started moving up the trail. "Did you and Eric pick a date yet?"

"Let's just say I'm close to convincing him that he wants a Valentine's Day wedding. But he's worried I'll need more time. And he might be right. I want a fancy dress, the kind that needs to be ordered months in advance."

"Lena, did you have a big wedding?" Katie asked. "With the traditional dress?"

"No." Lena focused on the dirt path. "My ex and I were married at city hall near West Point. He was a few years ahead of me and graduating."

"He was in the army too?" Katie said.

"He's an engineer. I met Malcolm at a West Point football game. He came down from his tiny liberal arts college, and, well, I think the allure of someone not tied to the military drew me in. Five months later, my dad met him and hated him, so I figured it was true love. We got married in a quick ceremony at town hall when he graduated, the year before my junior year."

"And it wasn't true love?" Georgia asked.

"It was," Lena admitted. "I loved him so much."

But love doesn't always last, she thought. If she wanted to rebuild her life on solid ground, she needed to concentrate on things that lasted, not the ones destined for failure.

"But he couldn't handle your PTSD," Georgia said, slowing the pace. "Could he?"

"No, I guess not," she said. "He kept expecting it would get better. But for those first six months home, I stepped further and further away from the life he'd imagined for us."

Hero brushed against her leg and her hand touched his golden fur. Side by side with her dog, she searched for the words, wanting to explain to these women who'd welcomed her into their lives how her day-to-day existence had crumbled that first year back.

"Malcolm had built a life in Portland," she continued. "He had friends. But they were so far removed from my reality while I was deployed. It was like there was a barrier dividing me from them. I felt numb. Sometimes it was as if I could see how his life would go on without me. And I felt horrible for thinking those thoughts because I'd survived a war when others hadn't . . ."

"Depressing, isn't it?" Georgia murmured.

"Yes," Lena said. "Eventually I found a way to move on. I started therapy and I got Hero. But months had passed by then. And Malcolm, he hadn't planned on waiting that long."

"He's a jerk," Katie said firmly.

"No, he tried. But he would kiss me and . . . and it was as if he was asking for something I couldn't give. He wanted me to be his wife, but I couldn't do it. Kisses, hugs, those everyday signs of affection felt so meaningless. I couldn't stand that feeling. So I pushed him away."

Lena paused on the trail and withdrew her water bottle. "How much further?"

"We're almost there," Georgia said. "Promise."

Almost there—wasn't that the story of her life these days? She'd come so far, learning what triggered her anxiety and putting coping mechanisms in place. But if she wanted to reach the pinnacle, she had to keep climbing.

"I'm sorry you're going through this," Katie said. "Listening to the two of you, my life seems so easy and normal. What you've lived through, and what you're living with now, amazes me."

"Don't discount normal, Katie," Lena said quietly. "Because that is where I'm headed and I'm going to get there. One day."

TWO HOURS LATER, as the sun rose high in the sky, Lena steered her truck down Katie's driveway, heading to her borrowed home.

"Thanks for giving me a ride," Katie said. "My brothers are going to lose it when they find out my wagon wouldn't start. They've been after me to get a new car, maybe a pickup, ever since Moore Timber cut the check to purchase our family's trucking business."

"It's nice that they look out for you," Lena said.

"Sometimes. Most of the time it is just annoying." Katie leaned forward. "Wow, look at that. Lena, I'll eat my words if my brothers went out and bought me a midnight blue convertible."

"Mercedes convertible?" Lena asked, scanning the parking area, because the details mattered, especially when it came to unfamiliar cars at her temporary home.

"I think so," Katie said.

Lena hit the brake. Hard. Parked beside the barn was a midnight blue Mercedes convertible. Once upon a time, she'd driven that car, loving the feel of the wind in her hair. But that was back when her life had felt like a fairy tale.

"Oh, and look, it came with a hot guy in a suit," Katie added. "You know, I don't think this is a present from my brothers. Or Liam."

"No." Lena put the truck in park and opened her door. "It belongs to Malcolm. My ex. I don't know how he found me here."

She climbed down with Hero following close behind her. As soon as they were out of the truck, Hero moved in front of her, demanding to take the lead, his yellow duck clutched tight between his teeth.

"Lena, wait," Katie called. "Should I get my brothers?"

"No." Lena held her head high following her dog. "Malcolm's harmless. I just wasn't expecting him."

"If you're sure," Katie said, eyeing Malcolm as if trying to assess whether the tall, lean man with the boyish good looks and expensive clothes that screamed, *Tech nerd* was a threat.

"I am," Lena said. "Why don't you head inside?"

Katie gave Malcolm a little wave and turned to the main farmhouse. Knowing it was only a matter of time before one of the Summers brothers appeared—Katie would send them despite Lena's reassurances—Lena approached her ex-husband. She stopped a few feet away, allowing enough space for Hero to stand between them.

"Hi Lena." He offered the goofy grin that once had the power to make her knees weak and her heart race. "I tried calling, but you turned off your cell."

"I'm thinking about changing providers. There's not a lot of service out here."

While that might be true, her phone had been turned off when she'd stopped paying the bill. But if she told her ex, he'd try to write her a check or offer alimony payments again. She needed the cash, but her foolish pride stood in the way. She'd pushed a decent man away, ending their marriage because she'd succumbed to post-traumatic stress. Yes, he'd been impatient. But a year was a long time to wait. And he'd already put in the time while she served her country. He'd thought the waiting was over when she left after fulfilling her five-year commitment to the army. She had too. And then she'd fallen apart. That was on her. Malcolm didn't owe her anything.

"Yeah, you're kind of in the middle of nowhere," he said.

"It's not that far from Portland," she said, falling into her defensive habits. "You found your way here."

"I guess not." He looked past her to the mountain peaks in the distance. "Nice views."

She crossed her arms in front of her chest. Hero moved closer, keeping his canine eyes focused on her ex. "What are you doing here, Malcolm?"

"This came for you." He stepped forward, holding out a large manila envelope. "You're being awarded a Silver Star."

"What?" Shocked, she took the envelope. "For what?"

"I didn't read it. A woman from the army called the house and told me. She said the vice-president is coming to an Oregon base next month to present the medal to you. Just you. When this came, well, I thought you would want it so I drove down, asked around town, and found you."

"Thank you." She stared down at the sealed envelope. A Silver Star. The army's third highest honor, and rarely given to a woman. Why had they picked her? The memory descended swift and fierce.

Gunfire. Men, and some women, but mostly men screaming. The noise was deafening. She'd raced to the front lines carrying important information before, but she'd never seen anything like this. These soldiers were dying. Unless someone carried them to safety. . .

"Lena, someone is coming this way." She could tell from his gentle tone that Malcolm was trying to warn her. "From the house," he added.

She glanced over her shoulder and spotted Chad, striding toward them. He moved with purpose, but his expression remained calm and easygoing.

"Hey Lena," he said, stopping at her side, offering her a smile. "Heard you hiked up to the falls today. Nice right?"

"Beautiful," she murmured, her mind shifting to the

present, the peace and quiet of Independence Falls, and the reassuring tone of Chad's voice.

"That's one of my favorite places," Chad said. "Now how about introducing me to your friend?"

Her hand went to Hero's fur as she made the introductions, her gaze moving back and forth between her ex and the man she'd threatened to shoot for climbing into bed with her last night.

"I drove down to give Lena her mail," Malcolm explained. "But I should probably hit the road. I need to get back to Portland and set up for poker. Remember our weekly games, Lena? With the crew?"

"I remember," she said. It had been years since she'd played, but she recalled the people who'd been her friends when she first moved to Portland, before she deployed—before her marriage dissolved.

Malcolm moved toward her and she stiffened. Hero stepped forward, ready and willing to create space for her. But her hand reached out and took hold of Chad.

And then she could breathe again. She hadn't realized she'd been holding her breath until the anxiety slipped away. Chad didn't move a muscle. He simply let her hold his hand as if it were a normal, everyday thing, and not a miracle in her war-torn world.

Malcolm's gaze dropped to their joined hands. And he knew. She could see it in his eyes. Her ex knew that the man standing beside her had touched her, held her, maybe more. There was a question mark there too, shining in his familiar face. If this man she'd known for a matter of hours could hold her hand, why did she shy away from the one who'd been her lover, who'd done his best to support her in those first few months home?

Because she'd been too broken, too different—and Malcolm's best hadn't been enough.

"Lena?"

Dropping Chad's hand, she gave her head a quick shake. She didn't have an answer to his unspoken question.

"OK," Malcolm said, stepping back. "OK, Lena. I'll head out now. But please think about it. It's a Silver Star, given by the vice president. After all you've been through, I think you should go to the ceremony and let them honor you. You earned this."

She nodded. "I'll think about it."

"And Lena." Her ex hesitated, glancing at the ground. She waited for him to say the words: *Come home.* Now that he had evidence that she'd pushed past the barrier that had driven them apart. Now that she could allow someone to share her space and touch her hand.

But I still can't let you in, she thought. They'd suffered together, trying to find a way through her mounting fears in those first months. But in the end, they'd had nothing left but frustration when she'd failed to meet the timeline in Malcolm's mind for her recovery.

"Your father called and left a message at the house. He's going to the ceremony with your brother and mother." Malcolm looked up at her. "Do me a favor and call them. Give them your new number when you get one, and your address. They're worried about you too."

"I will."

Malcolm turned and headed to his car. He paused by the door. "Bye, Lena. Take care of yourself."

"Good-bye."

Her mind pushed her ex-husband into the past, focusing on her present. Chad Summers. She owed him an explanation, one she didn't feel like giving. Slowly, she turned to him, noting the amused twinkle in his brown eyes.

"So," he said, rocking back on his heels. "You thought I was your dog there for a second, didn't you?"

Chapter 5

LENA LAUGHED, AND Chad knew he'd picked the right words. A smiling, amused woman placed him squarely within his comfort zone. But he couldn't stay within the boundaries. Her ex had sought her out on his land. And she hadn't looked overjoyed to see him.

"Your unexpected visitor must have shaken you if you reached for me," Chad said. "Anything I need to worry about?"

Her smiled faded. "Malcolm won't be coming back. Believe me. He gave up on me a while ago. He was probably just annoyed my parents were calling him."

"All right then," he said, shoving his hands in his jeans' pockets to keeping from brushing a loose strand of hair out of her face. He'd keep an eye out for her ex and ask Brody to do the same, but beyond that, he'd take her at her word. She didn't seem the type to bury her problems. She faced them head-on with a dog at her side.

And now him.

Last night, he'd left the studio apartment pretty damn certain she wouldn't want to touch him again. She'd allowed it the first time because she'd popped a sleeping pill. But unless she'd been sleepwalking on her hike to the falls, she was stone-cold sober today—and still she'd reached for his hand.

"So you won a medal?" He nodded to the envelope in her hands. "And the vice president is going to give it to you?"

"If I go to the ceremony," she said.

"Sounds like a pretty big deal. I have to agree with your friend in the fancy suit. You don't want to miss that."

"My family will be there." Her fingers clutched the envelope as if the thought of her relatives might leave her with hives. "They've had a hard time with my adjustment to being home."

His eyebrows shot up. Her family was having a hard time? She was the one who slept with a loaded gun at her side. Her relatives sounded like a bunch of jackasses, but he didn't think she'd appreciate his opinion. All families faced struggles. Shit, he knew that. And outside judgment didn't help.

"I don't like crowds. Or people touching me. Except you, I guess." She let out a mirthless laugh. "It must be your charm."

"You say that like it is a bad thing."

Her lips formed a thin line banishing every trace of her wry smile, along with the witty sense of humor he found pretty damn attractive. Not that he had any business adding to the things-I-like-about-Lena column.

"I'm the last thing you want in your life right now," she said.

"You don't know that." His trademark smile slipped. He wanted to fly a helicopter for Moore Timber. That was the number one item on his list. But the drop-dead gorgeous woman standing in front of him was nowhere near the last item. A relationship with a woman looking for a ring was close to the bottom, somewhere around double root canal. But he had a feeling diamonds didn't even make Lena's list of wants right now. Maybe that made her the perfect woman for him—apart from the fact that she'd turned a gun on him when he'd kissed her.

"I do," she said. "I want a lot of things I can't have, not until I piece my life back together."

She said the word "want" and his mind stumble-tripped back to last night. The way she'd responded to his touch . . . Yeah, he'd like to know a thing or two about her wants. But he wasn't a horny teenager anymore. He understood that her needs extended beyond the bedroom.

"What do you want, Lena?" he asked.

She pursed her lips as if debating what to tell him.

"Try the honest answer. I think I can handle it. I've got charm on my side, remember?"

"I'd like to leave the house without a dog at my side." Her voice started out soft and low as if she was worried someone—maybe the retriever chewing on his yellow duck at her feet—would overhear. But with each word, her tone grew stronger.

"I want to prove that I've moved on," she continued.

"To show everyone that I never gave up and I never will. A lot of people have given up on me, but I haven't given up on myself. I want a home. A job. A normal life. I want—" She drew her lower lip between her teeth. "I want all of the things you promised last night when you thought I was someone else."

Chad studied the too-serious expression on her beautiful face. How could anyone look at her and see someone who'd given up? But he had a feeling hearing it from him wouldn't help.

"I'd like to help you—"

"Why?" she demanded.

He shrugged. "Because you're pretty."

The look in her blue eyes called bullshit.

"OK, it's more than your looks. I want to help because I think you should have a home. And my sister would kick my ass if I didn't offer the apartment over the barn to you right now. So if you need a place to stay, you have one. For as long as it takes to get back on your feet."

"I can't afford to pay rent. Not yet. Not until I find a job."

The image of her ex's convertible flashed in his mind. Yeah, they'd split, but didn't the guy owe her something? But now wasn't the time or place to ask. "You'll find a job."

"It's not that easy," she said, glancing at Hero. He could see how it would hurt her chances to walk into an interview and start by explaining her fears. He had a bad feeling a lot of people, even strangers, would write her off before she said a word.

"Lena, I'm not one of the people who has given up on

you. My dad was in the army. I was just a kid when he got out, but . . . he was my hero. He's gone now, but I think he'd be pissed as hell if I didn't at least offer you a place to stay while you get back on your feet."

He saw tears threatening in her eyes and knew he should have kept his mouth shut about his dad. Before the dam broke and the teardrops started flowing, he backtracked to safer ground. "Maybe it's because I haven't known you long. But hey, Georgia and Katie seem to like you, so I'll give you the benefit of the doubt."

"Thank you," she said. Her voice wavered, but not a single tear fell.

"Hey now," he said. "Before you place me up on a pedestal beside your dog, aren't you going to ask if I have an ulterior motive?"

Suspicion replaced the awe and wonder in her blue eyes. Right now, she looked a lot like the woman he'd met by Eric's pond—wary, standoffish, and stunning. "Do you?"

Just a little problem I think you can help me solve, he thought. But she wasn't the answer to Eric's ultimatum. Still, that didn't mean he couldn't offer friendship.

"Have you had lunch?" he asked.

"No."

"How about a picnic? I'll make sandwiches." Her stomach rumbled. "Which I'm guessing you'll like."

She nodded and turned to her truck.

"Wrong way, Lena."

"If I'm going to be staying for a while, I need to bring my bag up." She unlocked the cover of her pickup and lowered the gate. Reaching inside, she withdrew a long duffel and set it on the ground. Then she pulled out a bag of dog food. Hoisting the puppy chow over her shoulder, she picked up the bag and headed for the door to the studio apartment.

"Need a hand with anything else?" he asked.

"No, this is everything."

Chad nodded and turned to the house with a sinking feeling that when she said "everything," she meant that all her possessions fit into that one bag. He glanced over his shoulder, watching as she disappeared up the stairs leading to the apartment above the barn, her dog at her heels. She was right to be suspicious, but this time he didn't have an ulterior motive.

He'd asked Lena to lunch because liked being around her, plain and simple.

SHOWERED AND DRESSED in a floor-length, sleeveless sundress, Lena buckled her sandals, slid her revolver into her purse, and grabbed a sweater, her stomach still rumbling. In spite of the noisy reminder, Chad's sandwiches weren't at the forefront of her mind.

Hand on the knob, she cast a backward glance at the envelope Malcolm had dropped off. The medal ceremony. Her family. The vice president. It was too much, too big. But it was also validation. If only she could walk up on that stage and allow the vice president of the country she'd served to pin a medal on her uniform in front of her family.

Hero nudged her free hand with his nose and she turned to the door. She'd come so far since that first month home when she'd gone to visit her parents in Texas and suffered her first nightmare. From there, it had been a downhill slide. But she was finding her way back. Today she'd reached for a man's hand. She'd wanted to touch someone. And holding on to Chad hadn't sent her spiraling into a panic attack.

She reached the bottom of the stairs and stepped outside, careful to lock the door behind her. "If that ceremony were next year, maybe I'd have a shot."

Because one touch didn't mean she was better. Of course, she could always test her theory by touching him again. Maybe his arms this time, to confirm if his biceps felt as good as they looked.

"Hungry?" Chad called as he crossed the parking area between the house and the barn, his cowboy boots kicking up dust with each step. He wore the same jeans and button-down flannel shirt he'd had on earlier, the sleeves rolled up. "I have turkey and cheese, mystery soy meat, and peanut butter and jelly."

"Mystery soy meat?"

"Katie's a vegetarian, so it is always in the house. Just in case you were too, I made one up. I'll eat anything. If you prefer meat, the real stuff is yours," he said, now halfway across the parking area.

She liked the way he started the conversation as he approached, giving her time to adjust to his presence. Hypervigilance was a bitch, and often left her feeling as if everyone around her was sneaking up on her.

"I eat meat, but I also like a good PB&J."

Chad stopped a few feet away, his easygoing trademark

grin in place. "I knew we had a lot in common. Ready to check out my favorite picnic spot?"

"Do we need to walk far?" She'd completed one hike today and had no intention of attempting a second.

"Nope." Chad turned and headed for the open field in the backyard. "Just past the clearing there is a good spot by a creek. Brody, Josh, and I camped out there when we were kids. Katie was too chicken to sleep in a tent all night."

"What was she afraid of?" she asked, following Chad across his backyard.

"Bugs mostly." He held back a low-lying branch and waited for her to step into the forest. "Don't worry, I brought spray."

"I wish there was a repellent for the things that scare me." She paused by a tree and waited for him to lead the way. He stayed true to his word, stopping not far from his backyard and pulling a blanket out of his backpack. She helped him spread it out on the ground, took a seat, and accepted a sandwich. "If I could pull out a spray bottle and erase my fears . . ."

"Your dog would be out of a job," he said, nodding to the golden retriever who'd claimed a corner of his blanket, content to chew on his toy.

"True. But he might enjoy retirement."

"What frightens you, Lena?" He stretched his long legs in front of him, easing down on the blanket.

She let out a mirthless laugh. "I have a laundry list of triggers. Loud noises, people getting too close, intimate situations. My ex wasn't fond of that last one. He didn't like the fact that I braced for hugs as if insurgents were about to storm our house, or that I shied away from his touch."

"That's why he gave up on you?"

"Yes. But it wasn't his fault," she said before Chad joined his sister in labeling Malcolm a jerk.

"It doesn't sound like anyone is to blame, Lena. Some things just happen. Like my little brother getting hit in the head while helicopter logging. It was an accident. Sure, there were a million ways to prevent it. He could have stayed home that day. The pilots could have flown a different route, or the copilot could have paid better attention to what was happening on the ground. But you can't think that way."

He handed her a bottle of water. "I try to save my energy for the problems that I know are my fault. Right now, I can't fly until I fix my reputation or start a serious relationship."

"Relationship?" Lena focused on keeping her voice steady. She'd struggled with reading people even since she'd returned home. Her life while deployed had been drawn in black and white. Home felt more like a rainbow with the colors constantly shifting. But she'd come a long way in the past few months, far enough to know that helicopter logging and relationships did not go hand in hand.

"I was under the impression you'd banned that word from your vocabulary," she added.

"You're right." He smiled as if every word out of his mouth made perfect sense. "But it turns out, I need a girlfriend."

She listened as he explained how his position at Moore

Timber, and his dreams of helicopter logging, meant he needed to appear serious about one woman.

"Now I'm aware of the fact that this crazy situation is my fault. Hell, you saw the proof last night that I've earned my reputation," he added. "And fixing it? That's on me too. But what you're going through? You were just doing your job, Lena. The way I see it, the fears following you now aren't that much different than Josh's short-term memory loss. And I haven't met a single doctor or nurse who expects my little brother to solve his problems on his own."

Lena froze, the peanut butter from Chad's homemade sandwich stuck to the roof of her mouth. She'd spent months surrounded by people pushing her toward an imaginary timeline as if she could check the boxes one by one—therapy, service dog—and become the person she'd been before. She had the tools, now it was up to her to do the rest, to fix her troubled mind.

But out of all the people in Independence Falls, the man with the panty-melting smile didn't see it that way. Sitting here, eating a sandwich that desperately needed more jam to justify the label PB&J, her dog relaxed at her side, she felt as if who she was might be enough.

For now.

Tomorrow? She'd like to wake up one step closer to normal.

A plan formed in her mind as she took a sip of water. "Are you going to do it? Settle down?"

"I'm not interested in leading someone on who is hoping for a ring in a few months," Chad said. "But I need to do something."

"Helicopter logging means that much to you?"

"Yes." There was passion and fire behind that one word. "I told you about my dad, right?"

She nodded. The man had been his hero. His words stuck with her because her father was a Hero, capital H, to most people, but he'd never been hers.

"Flying a helicopter was his dream. But when he left the army and faced the fact that he had four mouths to feed, he stuck with the family trucking business. He still found a way to take me and my brothers up in a helicopter and teach us the ropes."

"You could enlist," she said. "The army is always looking for pilots."

Chad shook his head. "Logging is in my blood. This place, this land—I love it here. I know it doesn't sound like much of a dream, flying around the forest and hauling out trees, but it's mine."

Who was she to challenge a person's hopes and dreams? Lena slid another quarter of the more-peanut-butter-than-jelly sandwich out of the bag and took a bite. Her goals for the future included finding a job and maybe, if she could push past her fears, accepting a Silver Star for serving her country.

And finding her way back to that moment last night, when she'd hovered on the edge of an orgasm . . .

When he'd touched her, awakening her desires with his words, this charming man had offered a glimpse at what the future could hold for her. Maybe she was finally starting to recover from the shattering trauma of surviving in a war zone. Or maybe it was this man, and his wicked demands, that had delivered her one step closer to normal.

"What if you knew it was just for show? What if it was clear from the start that rings and promises were not part of the deal?" She lowered the sandwich to her lap, her gaze fixed on Chad's chiseled, too-good-to-be-true features. "What if I pretend to be your girlfriend?"

"A fake relationship?" Chad blinked and stole a quick glance at Hero as if checking in with her canine companion to see if she'd lost her mind before looking back at her. But her dog remained focused on his toy.

"We could go out on dates and hopefully change this town's perceptions of you. At least until you find a copilot."

"Lena, I appreciate the offer. But I'm not sure that's the best idea—"

"It is," she said. "Everyone sees me as damaged and untouchable. They would never guess it was just for show."

His brow furrowed. "You really want to do this? Go out to dinner with me and let Independence Falls think we're dating?"

"Yes. But I have an ulterior motive." She drew a deep breath. "I want our relationship to be real at night. When we're alone."

Chapter 6

CHAD FOCUSED ON the smudge of peanut butter on Lena's cheek. Nine times out of ten, he could read a woman's signals and follow her words, even if she said one thing and meant another. But with Lena, he needed clarification. It was like flying over a logging site. A little bit to the left led to trouble when you had a giant metal hook hanging down and a person on the ground trying to grab it.

"I'm going to need you to spell out what you're asking for," he said.

She looked him straight in the eyes. For the first time since he'd met this mysterious, intriguing woman by Eric's pond, he saw a soldier. The wealth of determination in her expression blew him away.

"I know last night didn't end well—"

"You're the first woman who has ever pulled a gun on me in the sack."

"You're the first man to touch me and leave me wishing

for more in nearly eighteen months," she countered. "More if you count the fourteen months I spent in Afghanistan."

"Wow," he muttered, his mouth full of fake meat. What the hell else was there to say to that? "Wait, you think I healed you?"

Because if she thought last night had ended well . . . shit, what the hell had her sex life been like before she'd gone to war?

"No. But you made me think I'm closer to normal," she said softly. "And that's my dream. I love Hero, but I hate the fact that I need him. And—"

She drew a deep breath, her gaze dropping to the blanket. He had a feeling there was so much more she wasn't telling him. "And we have chemistry. I want you to touch me and whisper dirty things in my ear."

Chad let out a slow breath, running his hands through his hair. "Lena, I'd like to help you. And for selfish reasons, I'd love to take you up on your offer. I want to fly almost as much as I want to breathe. But I'm not so sure I'm the right guy. I don't know the first thing about what you're going through. I never served. And aside from hanging out with Georgia, I don't know anything about PTSD."

"I'm not asking you to be my shrink," she said. "I have one of those. I want you to be my lover, or at least try. And I'll do my best to convince Independence Falls that we're dating. Of course, if the thought of sex with me turns you off—"

"No." He wanted to agree to her plan. It was as crazy as flying blind over a forest, but part of him wished he could make Lena *his*.

"If we do this," he said, in his best no-nonsense voice, "I don't set the limits. You do. Understood?"

She nodded.

"I'm game for anything. I want you, Lena. But I think we both know this is shaky ground. Promise me, you'll tell me no whenever you need to say the word. I don't need a reason. And I swear, I'll always listen."

"I promise." She held out her hand, her fingers trembling. "Then it's a deal?"

He gave her a gentle, quick handshake to seal their crazy plan before pulling back, allowing her space. "Deal. But I need you to promise me one more thing. When I'm in your bed, the gun is unloaded."

She smiled. "No loaded weapons in bed. I can do that."

He shook his head. Part of him knew this was wrong. She was hurting and he wasn't the man to help her. But part of him flat-out *wanted* her. "We might both regret this, but how about dinner tonight? I could pick you at five?"

"It's a date."

CHAD HAD SPENT more nights than he wanted to admit in the apartment over the barn. But he'd never knocked on the door holding a bunch of flowers and a gift bag. And he'd never been nervous.

"Hi." Lena opened the door wearing the same long dress she'd had on earlier. She'd added lip gloss, but one look told Chad he'd overdone it with the flowers.

"Hey." He offered his trademark smile, the one that

made most women melt. Except Lena. She drew her brows together, studying the offerings as if they were part of a foreign ritual she didn't understand.

"I'm ready to go," she said, still eyeing the flowers.

"May I come in first?" he asked. "Put these in water?"

"Of course." She stepped back from the door and turned to the stairs.

"What did you do this afternoon?" He followed her up to the studio. They reached the top step and Hero paused on the landing, glancing back at him. Chad smiled at the dog, but as with his owner, it didn't exactly lead to a doggie smile. The retriever just studied him for a moment longer before stepping into the studio.

"I spent the afternoon job hunting online at the library. And it was . . . discouraging."

"Not much out there?" he asked, knowing the answer.

"No."

They reached the apartment and he held out the bouquet. "Maybe these will brighten your day."

"I didn't realize fake relationships came with flowers and presents." She took the colorful arrangement, waiting for him to hand over the bag.

"This is just a little something to get us started," he said, holding it out of her reach. "For your side of the bargain."

She held out her hand. "Hand it over, Chad Summers."

Hoping he wasn't making a huge mistake, running their deal into the ground before they left his family's property, he gave her the pink gift bag. She set the flowers on the two-person table and pulled out the tissue paper. Then she reached inside, her blue eyes widening as she removed her present.

"You bought me a vibrator?" Lena turned the pink silicone sex toy over in her hands. "Thank you. But—"

"Lena." He reached out, careful not to touch her as he took the vibrator from her. "Let me show you why."

"Now?"

He nodded, his courage building. The way she looked at the toy in his hands, she wanted the pleasure it promised. After hearing her desperate moans, her pleas for a release that had remained out of reach because he hadn't known the rules of the game last night, he wanted to send her soaring. But this time, he refused to scare her.

"What about dinner?" she asked.

"We'll get there. The night is still young. And since I'm grounded until we find a copilot, I don't have anywhere to be at the crack of dawn tomorrow. Do you?"

"No. The library is not open on Sunday."

"Then we have all night," he said, making a mental note to offer the computer at the house for her job search. But he didn't want to distract her now, not when she was focusing on his hands. "Is your gun unloaded?"

"Yes," she said. "It's in my purse, but no bullets. And I can put Hero in the bathroom."

"That would be good." He glanced at the golden retriever sitting practically on his mistress's feet. Later, they would also talk about why she carried a revolver with her to dinner—and everywhere else. He had a long list of questions. Some she might not wish to answer, and that was fine by him. But he'd like to know if she had a permit to carry a concealed weapon.

After he found out what noises she made when she came.

"Once he's settled, come sit on the bed."

Lena obeyed, leading an unhappy Hero to the studio's bathroom. "Stay," she murmured to the dog through the hollow wood door. The dog whined as she crossed the room, selected one of the chairs from the two-person table, and positioned it in front of the door.

"In case he tries to break out," she said.

"Good thinking," he said. "Tomorrow, I'll fix the lock."

Lena walked over to the bed and sat, every muscle in her body visibly tense. She might as well have been settling into the dentist's chair.

"You don't have to do this now," she said. "We can go out first."

"Lena, right now, " he said, his voice low. "I'm going to make you come so hard you see stars and then I'll feed you."

"You do this for all your dates?" she asked, her tone laced with sarcasm, her gaze fixed on the toy in his hands.

"No. Now close your eyes." The lights were off in the small space, but the late afternoon/early evening sunlight poured in through the windows. And he welcomed it, wanting to see her and gauge her reactions. "I'm not going to touch you yet. I promise."

"OK." Eyes closed, her shoulders relaxed.

He stood in front of her, out of reach, but close enough

that she could hear every word as he turned the vibrator over in his hand. "I'm not going to lay a hand on you tonight, Lena. But I'd like to finish what we started. I want to watch your beautiful face as you come, see your body bend and arch from the pleasure. And I want to know I brought you there, even if I have to do it with a toy between us.

"Tell me no, tell me to stop if it is too much, and I will. But right now, I want you to keep your eyes closed and lift your skirt. I want you to tease me with your long legs, beautiful."

Eyes closed, head tilted back, her fingers clutched the fabric of her dress, slowly drawing it higher.

"That's it. Draw it out, make me want you," he murmured, his gaze fixed on her bare skin. "Tonight. Right now. This is for you. But know that I want you, Lena. Looking at you, the thought of giving you pleasure, hearing you cry out, it all makes me hard.

"Now lift your hips," he ordered. "I want your skirt at your waist."

Lena rocked back on her elbows, her hips lifting high off the bed, her breasts thrust upward as her body formed a plank. That position—*fuck*—if only he could toss the toy aside and run his hands up her legs, touching and exploring her.

"Like this?" she asked, lowering her hips to the bed, her long skirt hiding the curve of her slim waist. Her soft voice, devoid of fear, told him she was with him. Ready. *Wanting.*

"Yeah. Like that." His gaze narrowed in on her white

lacy underwear. "Did you wear those for me? Hoping I'd catch a glimpse under your skirt?"

"Yes," she gasped.

"Good answer. Now slip them off."

Raising her hips again, she wiggled the slip of lace off, kicking her panties away. Naked from the waist down, she leaned back on her elbows, her knees pressed together and her eyes closed.

Kneeling at her feet, he pressed a button and the vibrator moved in his hand, shaking and rotating. "Spread your legs, Lena. Let me see you. Spread them wide."

"Chad—"

"Take your time. I'm not going to touch you. Not with my hands. I just want to look at you. See if you're wet and ready. If you are, then, beautiful, I'm going to tease you with your new toy, let you feel the movement, waiting until you want more, until you ask for more," he said, spelling out his game plan, hoping to dispel her fears—and turning himself on in the process.

Slowly, her thighs parted, her feet heel-toeing apart. And, oh yeah, she was wet and ready.

"You're so damn beautiful, Lena." He inched closer, still on his knees. Fighting the urge to press his hands against her and bury his face between her spread legs, he touched the vibrator against her right thigh. She gasped, her back arching, her ass pressing into the bed as her legs moved together.

"Easy, Lena," he murmured, mesmerized by her movements. He couldn't remember ever taking a seduction this slow, watching his partner's desire unravel piece by piece.

It might be unusual, but it sure as hell worked for him. His cock agreed, pressing against his fly.

"Keep your legs apart," he said. "Unless you want me to stop."

"Don't stop," she said, obeying his instructions, her knees falling open again. He rewarded her, slowly moving the toy up her thigh until the rotating head was poised at her entrance. Running the tip over her, up and down, gently at first, and then with the slightest pressure, he teased her. He learned where she liked to be touched, listening to her moan as the vibrator toyed with her clit before moving lower.

"More," she said, that one word riding the boundary between command and plea. Her hands moved to her breasts, squeezing and pinching her nipples, as if trying to push herself closer to release.

"Oh hell, yeah," he said, his voice a low growl. He welcomed the help, loving the way her body responded to her touch.

He pressed the vibrator inside her, watching the first inch disappear, then another, and another. Easing it in and out, he mimicked the thrusting motion his hips would make if he were inside her. Part of him wished it was his cock making her moan, her fingers falling away from her breasts and digging into the blankets. But damn, he loved watching her.

"I'm going to make you come now, Lena."

SHE CLUNG TO his words, wanting to believe him. Chad had stayed true to every promise he'd made her so far. He hadn't touched her, using the low, gravelly sound of his voice to connect the pulsing sensations racing through her body to the man kneeling between her splayed legs. But it was his respect for her boundaries, more than his dirty talk, that allowed her to open up, and really, truly feel the pleasure, the stirring of an orgasm, bigger and bolder than one delivered by her fingers.

Her world had been divided for eighteen long months between the things she could have and everything else. And now, with his words inciting her senses, and the vibrations whipping her body into a frenzy, her world was a riot of rushing, blending feelings.

Her hips bucked, seeking more. And he gave it to her, quickening the pace of his thrusts.

"That's it, beautiful, let go," he murmured. "Come for me. I'm dying here, waiting to hear the sounds you make when you explode."

She moaned and arched, feeling her muscles tense around the silicone penis as it shook inside her. He pulled it back, thrusting it in one last time, holding it there as she fell apart.

"More," she pleaded, too far lost in her orgasm to know what she was begging for. She just did not want this to end. The vibrator moved in her, pulling back, then pushing forward, so deep she felt his hand against her skin. She opened her eyes, the orgasm spiraling higher and higher, propelled by his touch.

Lifting her head, gasping for breath, she clung to the sheets. Chad stared back at her as if he wanted to stay kneeling between her legs, driving her wild. Hunger, need—it was all there in his brown eyes.

The orgasm ended and her heartbeat raced. But it wasn't anxiety rearing its ugly head. Not this time. She'd reached the finish line. Maybe, just maybe, she was one step closer to the woman she'd been before her journey halfway around the world.

Lena closed her eyes, resting her head back on the bed. The swell of nerves that had bubbled up as she'd read the blatant need written in his expression . . . that wasn't fear. Her world had been bookended by anxiety for months now, and it didn't feel like this.

She felt him move away. The buzzing stopped. He'd turned off the toy. Opening her eyes, she stared at the ceiling wondering what to say to her pretend boyfriend, the man who'd delivered her first orgasm in mixed company in many, many months.

"Lena?" His voice was soft and gentle, devoid of the naughty edge that slipped in when he issued commands.

"Hmm?" she murmured.

"You're not thinking about your gun, are you?"

She laughed, propping herself up her elbows. He'd set the toy aside and stood with his hands in his pockets, watching her with his trademark charming smile in place. "No. I'm still too shaky to handle firearms."

He nodded, his smile fading. "You would tell me if it was too much, right?"

"It wasn't." She sat up, smoothing her skirts down over her legs. "It was different, but lovely."

"We need to work on your vocabulary."

Lena pressed her lips together, searching for the right word. She glanced at the vibrator on the nightstand. "It was perfect," she said. "For me."

"So I get a gold star for creativity?"

"Yes." She smiled, suppressing a giggle. What was it about this man? She'd laughed more with him in two days than she had in so long. Most people tiptoed around her, their expressions grim and their actions wary. Maybe she'd needed that for a while. But Chad brushed past her barriers, delivering sweet-talking charm and humor. And the words he used when he set aside the sweet . . .

Tonight. Right now. This is for you. But know that I want you, Lena. Looking at you, the thought of giving you pleasure, hearing you cry out, it all makes me hard.

Oh yes, this man deserved a gold star.

"We'll start a sticker chart for you after dinner." She moved the chair and opened the bathroom door, freeing her disgruntled dog. "Good boy, Hero," she murmured to the retriever.

"If you two are ready, let's get something to eat and show this town you're mine," Chad said. "Because Lena, right now, with your I-just-got-out-of-bed glow, you look like you belong with me."

Chapter 7

LENA STUDIED CHAD'S fluid, easy movements as he steered his pickup down into Independence Falls. Hero sat between them on the front bench, but Chad didn't seem to mind. He had to be uncomfortable, and not just because there was a golden retriever breathing in his ear.

She wasn't the only one turned on by his experiment with the pink toy. But she'd left the room satisfied, her body still tingling. She'd been trained to pay attention to details and she'd seen the way he adjusted himself when he thought she wasn't looking.

"Are you all right?" she asked. "Do you want to turn back, take a little break before dinner? I know you're probably eager to get your part of our deal in motion, but if you need a few minutes, I understand."

He cast a sideways glance at her before turning his attention back to the road. "Lena, did you just ask me if I need to jerk off?"

"Yes."

He flashed a devilish grin, his eyes lit with amusement. "Would you like to watch?"

Yes. No. "Maybe?"

Chad laughed. "If you'd said yes, I might have turned the truck around. But I think I can keep it together long enough to get you fed. I appreciate the thought."

"You're welcome." She folded her arms across her chest. "And I think I might like to watch one day. I think there are a lot of things I might want to try."

"Stop teasing the man with the hard-on who wants to buy you dinner."

She smiled at the playful note in his voice. "I'll do my best. Where are we going?"

"What do you like to eat?" He slowed the truck as they approached Main Street. The strip was lined with storefronts, a church on each corner, and a few restaurants. On one side of the street, the buildings touched, but across the pavement the lots had green spaces in between. And many of the restaurants used the grassy areas to set up outdoor seating.

"I'm not picky," she said. *About food.* Cramped indoor seating might ruin his plan. It would be hard to date a woman who refused to enter the restaurant—or worse, caused a scene when she bolted two minutes after entering, a full-blown panic attack nipping at her heels along with her dog.

"Pizza? A Slice of Independence has picnic tables outside."

"Outdoors would be nice." Lena exhaled, feeling as

if she'd been holding her breath, waiting to take a shot at a target. One orgasm courtesy of a pink penis did not mean she was ready for a crowded restaurant on a Saturday night. "And I like pizza. Is it good?"

"It's the only pizza joint in town, so I'd say it's the best there is." He turned into the half-filled parking lot, cut the engine, and hopped out. He was at her door opening it before she'd released her seat belt. "Why don't you grab a table and I'll go inside and place the order? Any requests, or are you willing to take a gamble on the special pie of the day?"

"The special. Unless it has mushrooms."

Lena selected an empty red picnic table on the outskirts of the grassy seat-yourself area. A family with two young kids, one barely walking and another that looked to be about the same age as Nate, Eric's nephew, sat close to the door. Nearby, a young couple, probably still in high school, were splitting a pie. The seating area was visible from the street and cars occasionally slowed down to wave.

Lena had to give him credit. Chad had picked the perfect spot. No crowds or noisy interior, plenty of space for her dog to lounge in the grass, yet still in full view of Independence Falls on a Saturday night.

About ten minutes later, the screen door attached to the side of the brick building swung open and Chad walked out carrying a pizza, a stand, and a couple of plates. He smiled and called out a greeting to the family as he made his way to the table.

"Trish is the only server working tonight and she's slammed with customers inside, so I offered to play waiter."

Chad set up the stand on one side of the table and placed the pizza on it. "Sorry to keep you waiting."

"I don't mind." She reached for a plate. "What are we having?"

"The special had mushrooms, so I went traditional. Plain cheese on half and pepperoni on the other side," he said. "Dig in. I'm going to run inside for our waters. Unless you want something stronger. A soda maybe? Or a lemonade?"

"Water is fine." She selected a slice of plain cheese and let it cool on her plate.

Returning with the waters, Chad sat on the bench across from her. The young couple and the family stared at her, as if trying to figure out who she was. On the street, a car slowed, the raven-haired twenty-something driver nearly swerving off the road.

"I feel like I'm eating in front of an audience," she said, her voice low.

"It's been a long time since I've brought a date here," he said.

"How long?"

"Freshman year of high school."

She froze the pizza at her lips. "You gave up on dating that early?"

"I'm kidding, Lena. It hasn't been that long. A couple of years maybe." He nodded to her dog. "Does Hero need a slice?"

She shook her head, getting the hint. He didn't want to talk about it. And she didn't want to push. Her fake boyfriend's dating history was none of her concern, especially when she had a mouth full of the best pizza she'd had in years. "No. He's fine with dog food."

Her dog dropped his yellow duck toy and let out a bark as if he understood the words "dog" and "food" pertained to him. But she ignored him.

"I would hate to waste this on an animal that mistakes a chair leg for dinner," she said. "The crust is perfect. Not too thin. Not too thick. I haven't had a pizza like this since I lived in New York."

"In the city?" He selected a slice of the pepperoni.

"No. Upstate. I went to West Point."

"You always knew you wanted to be in the army?"

"My father always knew he wanted me to follow in his footsteps and be in the army," she corrected.

"Your dad served?"

She nodded, sliding a second slice onto her plate. "And my brother. He fought in Iraq."

"That must have been hard for your parents," Chad said, leaning back. "To watch both their kids go to war."

No, it was what they'd wanted for their children, Lena thought, biting into the oh-so-perfect crust. Maybe not the war in the Middle East. But wearing the uniform? That had been their dream from day one.

"My brother was home by the time I graduated and deployed," she said. There was so much more to the story, but she wasn't ready to share the details yet.

"Your family must be proud of you." She could feel Chad watching her carefully. "For receiving a Silver Star."

"I'm sure they are. My dad grew up very poor. His parents moved to Texas from Mexico when he was about ten. They became citizens, my dad went to school, and my grandfather's business thrived. They love this country. As soon as my dad was old enough, he enlisted, determined to serve. He dreamed about sending his kids to military schools, but my brother followed in his footsteps, enlisting when he turned eighteen. The day I graduated from West Point, my father cried. He was so proud of me."

Chad set his half-eaten slice on his plate. "Lena, you can tell me to mind my own business if you want, but why aren't they helping you now?"

"They don't understand," she said. "There's nothing wrong with me. Physically. But I refuse to go back and serve another tour. I'm done. I don't think they could accept that. They didn't understand.

"Maybe if there was one event that I could point to and say this why I can't move forward with my life. But it's not isolated to the images in my nightmares. Waking up every day not knowing if someone will attack your unit. Wondering about IEDs every time you get into a truck or go out on patrol . . . it builds and builds until your normal is fear."

She selected another slice of piece. "*My* normal is fear right now. It wasn't like that for my brother or father. Their injuries healed, to the extent they ever will, following the timeline set out by their doctors. My family expected the same would be true for me."

"So they gave up on you," he said. "Like your ex?"

"You're awfully nosy for a fake boyfriend."

"Just hard to imagine walking away from you, Lena. You're beautiful and fascinating. And you must have done some pretty amazing stuff over there to receive a medal from the vice president." Chad offered her another slice of pepperoni pizza, but she shook her head. "Plus your ex drove all the way down here to give you that envelope."

"Malcolm isn't a bad guy," she said quietly.

"Look, Lena," Chad said slowly, humor fading from his brown eyes. "If there's a chance you can fix things with him, I don't want to be in the way."

"No," she said flatly. "There's no chance. Even if there were, I don't want to go back. Malcolm had an imaginary line of how much he could take before he gave up. We blew past his idea of when my recovery should've ended months ago."

"Chad!" A shrill female voice burst the bubble around her, Chad, and their too-serious conversation.

Lena turned her head, spotting a slim, tall woman with black hair styled into a spiked pixie cut. Ms. Pixie approached the picnic bench and stopped beside Chad.

"We missed you at the bar last night," the woman said. "It didn't feel like a Friday night without you."

"Yeah, sorry," he said. "I had something."

"Forgiven." Ms. Pixie rested her hand on Chad's arm.

"Delilah, this is Lena," Chad said, carefully withdrawing his arm from the other woman's hold. He reached for his water, nodding in her direction. "She just moved to Independence Falls. Lena, meet Delilah Travis."

Ms. Pixie's eyes narrowed as she studied Lena. Could the other woman see her "glow"? The thought sent a tingling reminder of what they'd done on her borrowed bed before heading to dinner. And how she'd felt doing it . . .

Amazing. Orgasmic. Glowing.

"Welcome to Independence Falls," Ms. Pixie said, turning back to Chad. "I stopped in to see Josh today at the end of my shift."

"How was he?" Chad said, glancing across the table to add: "Delilah's a nurse at the hospital."

"He was giving one of his nurses a hard time about the food. Something about too many vegetables and not enough meat."

Chad grinned. "Sounds like my brother."

"The nurse tried to explain that he placed the order yesterday. It's too bad about his memory," Delilah said, shaking her head.

"I'm just glad he's here with us," Chad said. "Maybe he can't remember marking those silly hospital menu cards, but he still knows he'd rather have a bacon double cheeseburger than anything they offer."

"Everyone in Independence Falls is praying for Josh and hoping he makes a full recovery," Delilah said. "I heard Eric threw a little party for you and your brothers. Awfully sweet of him what with all the wedding planning on his plate right now."

"I don't think he's handling much of the planning," Chad said. "I would bet that is all on Georgia."

"I heard," Delilah said, dropping her voice low, "that Georgia moved up the date."

"I wouldn't know. Eric and I don't spend much time talking flowers and I-dos, you know? But Lena might. She's a friend of Georgia's. And from what I understand, she's had a hand in the planning."

Lena debated kicking him under the table.

Ms. Pixie turned to her, head cocked to one side. "Is it true? I'd heard spring, but now it might be a winter wedding?"

"I don't think Georgia has made a decision," Lena said.

The other woman pursed her lips as if debating whether Lena was hiding the truth.

"I'm sure it will depend on Eric's schedule," Lena added, though she suspected that in this case, the groom would gladly hand over the running of his multimillion-dollar timber operation if his fiancée decided they should wed today.

"If you need a date," Ms. Pixie said, her hand returning to Chad's arm as she gave him a squeeze, "you have my number."

"I'm sure Georgia will want to keep it small. I probably won't make the invitation list. But if they do, I think I'm covered." Chad winked at her, before turning back to the woman holding his arm. "Delilah, you might want to place your order for the special before they run out."

The other woman nodded, releasing Chad as she stepped away. "I'll see you around."

Lena watched Ms. Pixie walk away. "Wow, she is . . ."

"Forward?" Chad supplied.

She touched you like she'd seen you naked and wanted you to remember the moment, Lena thought. "At least she didn't pour a beer over your head."

"Hey now, most people like me," Chad said.

"Here there, stranger!"

Lena looked up and spotted a blonde approaching their

picnic table, a second woman following behind her. Both women were focused on Chad, their smiles wide and welcoming.

She glanced back at her "date." The man was good-looking, but he wasn't a god. And from what she'd seen, this town was littered with ripped, muscular men. They could make a "Bad Boys of Logging" calendar and easily fill every month.

Or maybe not. Eric and Liam had pristine reputations as far as she knew. Sure, they were off the market now. But based on what she'd learned from Georgia, Eric had been devoted to his nephew before falling in love, and still treated the child who'd lost both parents as his own. Lena has a feeling no one in Independence Falls would label him a "bad boy."

But Chad? He had bad boy written all over him.

Lena waited until the last member of the Chad Summers Fan Club moved out of earshot. "I can see why you don't take women out," she teased. "You probably have longer conversations in bed."

"It's only a conversation if you say wicked, naughty things back to me, beautiful," Chad said. The nice-guy smile he'd worn for the others vanished, replaced by a don't-tempt-me grin.

Her breasts responded to his words, tightening, hoping for a touch, a kiss—something. The need rippled through her, moving lower.

"A good listener is an important part of any conversation," she said, smiling as if her entire body wasn't vibrating with a foreign feeling—the need to reach for him. She folded her hands in her lap. "Just something I learned in the army."

"Yeah, did they also teach you to take orders?"

The low growl of his voice coupled with those words—if Ms. Pixie and friends could hear him now, they'd probably faint at his feet.

"I was an officer. I gave the orders," she said, feeling as if she was teasing a lion. But he was her lion until they convinced the town he'd shredded the reputation that drew women to him like moths to light.

"Lena, I'm listening. Any time you want to take charge."

The way he looked at her . . . it was as potent as if he'd run his hands over her bare skin. Her heartbeat sped up and she debated ordering him to march back to his truck, drive her home, and take her to bed. And maybe this time, she'd leave the pink toy on the nightstand.

Maybe.

She raised one hand, instantly feeling something soft and furry. It was Hero, checking in, his front paws resting on the picnic bench beside her. Turning her hand over, she stroked his golden coat. Maybe she was getting ahead of herself. Even if she wanted to, she couldn't stake a claim based on one orgasm and a fake date. Chad wasn't hers any more than he belonged to the ladies of his fan club.

"Do they drive in from other towns to see you?" she asked.

Chad leaned back, palms flat on the table. "Who?"

"I've met more single women tonight in small-town Oregon then I recall seeing out in Portland on a Saturday night."

Chad shook his head. "You're funny."

She'd been labeled a lot of things since she returned home and left the army, but never funny.

"And no, they're all locals. I went to high school with Delilah. Some of the other ladies you met too." Chad stood, picking up the empty plates and pizza tray. "Did you save room for dessert? They have chocolate and vanilla soft serve."

"Can they do a swirl?" she asked. The thought of ice cream and pizza all in one night—she was ready to sign up for more fake dates. "In a cone?"

"Yes, Lena. They do." His gaze dropped to her mouth. "And I have a feeling I'm going to enjoy watching you eat ice cream."

Chapter 8

Chad ordered the ice cream and stepped to the side, glancing out the window. With the sun starting to slip behind the mountains, they had an hour or so before darkness descended on A Slice of Independence's picnic tables—plenty of time to eat their cones before heading home. Hell, he didn't think he could handle more than sixty minutes of curious old friends stopping by to say hello.

But Lena? She hadn't balked at the parade of women who'd approached their table. He had an oh-shit moment when he spotted Delilah, wondering if his date would panic. Lena had remained calm. And after the parade wandered away, playful.

Through the window, he watched as she knelt in the grass beside her golden retriever, rubbing the dog's belly. Her long hair felt forward, obscuring her face. The wanting, which had been building inside him since he knocked on her door holding the flowers and her present, rose up, pretty freaking literally. He wished he could take her back to the apartment over the barn and climb into bed with her. They could take turns giving orders, or maybe he'd let her call the shots tonight. Anything to get to the place where she screamed his name as she came, her picture-perfect body lost in pleasure.

"Chad," Trish called from behind the counter. "Think you can stop staring at your friend long enough to take your cones?"

He turned away from the window and took the ice cream, smiling at the waitress only a few years his junior. "Thanks."

With a cone in each hand, he headed for his date, searching for Lena through the screen door. She was still on the ground with her dog. Out of the corner of his eye, he spotted three children racing through the grass. Chad frowned. They were heading for Lena, coming at her from behind. For a split second, he debated calling out to her. But then the kids rushed past.

From the doorway to the pizza place, he watched tension ripple through her body.

Hero went from blissed-out dog to protector, springing to all fours, pressing close to his owner. Her arms wrapped around the animal, her shoulders trembling, her head turning left to right as if scanning the area for the threat. He saw the moment her gaze landed on the kids. Her eyes closed and she buried her face in Hero's soft fur.

She looked so damn alone, clutching her dog. How hard was it to move through each day knowing that the movement of innocent children playing outside might ignite old fears? It took a helluva lot, he realized, to keep pushing forward, to hold out for a future, and to maintain her witty sense of humor in the process.

Chad turned away from the door and returned to the counter. "Trish, can you hold these for a minute? And can you get me a piece of paper and a pen?"

The exasperated waitress behind the counter gave him a you-can't-be-serious look.

"Please?" he added, flashing his signature smile.

Trish shook her head. "For you, Chad, sure."

She slipped a pad of paper used for taking orders and a pencil across the counter, and then held out her hands to take the cones. "But make it quick. We're slammed here. And these cones will melt soon."

Chad picked up the pencil and started writing.

I want dibs on calling the shots, beautiful. I want to watch you lick your chocolate/vanilla swirl and imagine you on your knees, your mouth working its magic.

He folded the paper three times and slid it across the counter to Trish. "I'll take the cones. Would you mind dropping that note off with my date?"

Trish nodded to the filled restaurant as she handed over the cones. "Chad, we have a full dining room."

"I don't see any food waiting in the window," he said. "Please Trish? I'll double your tip."

"You're headed out there," the waitress challenged. "Why do you need me to deliver a note first?"

"Because it will make her smile." Chad glanced out the window. Lena had returned to the bench, but Hero remained at her side. There wasn't a hint of joy on her pretty face. "And maybe laugh."

Trish picked up the piece of paper. "Fine. I'll do it."

Chad waited by the door, tracking the waitress's movements as she hurried to the table. Trish smiled at Lena, set the note beside her, and cleared the remaining dirty dishes. Confusion chased by concern flickered in Lena's eyes. And then she unfolded the paper.

Her cheeks turned pink and her eyes widened. And then she laughed. Chad stepped out the door, grinning like fool as melted ice cream ran over his hands. He liked Lena just like that—hot, flushed, and laughing.

"Here's your cone." He stopped beside the picnic table, holding it out to her.

She took the dripping treat and raised it to her lips. Her tongue ran around the base, licking up the drips. Once. Twice.

Shit, he needed to sit down before he fell to his knees and begged her not to stop. He wanted to watch her eat ice cream all night.

Lena glanced up at him, her lips hovering over the cone. "I haven't done this in a while."

"You need instructions?" Chad claimed his seat on the bench, his frozen treat still dripping. Right now, he didn't care if it formed a puddle on the table.

"I'm listening," she said.

"Start at the bottom."

Her wide blue eyes stared back at him over the top of

her treat as her tongue obeyed his orders. Watching her, he wished he could toss her over his shoulder, carry her to his truck, and beg her to treat his cock like an ice cream cone.

"Swirl your tongue up to the top," he continued, keeping his voice low, not wanting anyone to overhear his raw, needy words. "Wrap your lips around the top. Keep working your tongue, beautiful. And suck."

She closed her eyes and he swore he heard her moan.

"Ah hell, Lena, I'm going to buy you ice cream very damn day just to watch you enjoy it."

She laughed, licking up the drips before nodding to the melted disaster in his hand. "You should start on yours before it disappears."

"Yeah, I'd rather—"

"Chad!"

A booming male voice that he'd heard one too many times playing flag football in high school shattered the moment. Chad spotted two guys winding their way through the tables. To call them friends would be stretching the definition of the word. But Tim filled in for Eric's crew chiefs when needed. He'd graduated Independence High a year behind Chad and was young for the job. Being the Bull of the Woods came with a fair amount of responsibility, and demanded respect—at least when they were on a job site.

During the off hours? Not so much. Tim and his sidekick, Peyton, enjoyed their share of recreational substances. One look at the pair, and Chad had a bad feeling the guys were high as a freaking kite right now.

"Hey." Chad greeted them. "I figured you guys would

be harvesting that tract of land up near The Dalles for another week."

"Nope, finished yesterday and spent today driving home," Peyton, the larger of the two guys, said, stopping in front of their table. Yeah, the men had clearly been smoking something before stopping for pizza.

"We could work faster with a helicopter hauling the logs out," Tim pointed out, his lips forming a smirk reminiscent of grade school bullies on the playground. Chad had stood up for enough kids to know the look.

"Yeah, yeah, we're working on getting the new bird up in the air," Chad said, turning to Lena. "Guys, this is Lena. She just moved to the area. Lena, meet Tim"—Chad pointed to the shorter man—"and Peyton." He indicated the larger man. "These guys work on one of Eric's crews."

"Welcome to Independence Falls." Peyton offered Lena a goofy smile, and Chad's jaw tightened. He wanted this conversation over. Now.

"Did you guys try the pie of the day?" Tim asked.

"Nope," Chad said. "It had mushrooms and Lena is not a fan. But if you head inside and talk to Trish, I'm sure she'll hook you up."

"No shrooms?" Peyton said, his bloodshot eyes widening. "What if someone held a gun to your head and ordered you to eat a mushroom?"

Chad opened his mouth to tell Tweedledee and Tweedledum to go inside and order their damn dinner.

"I'd take the gun away," Lena said simply before returning to her ice cream

And just like that another oh-shit moment faded away.

"She's a marksman," Chad added. "Served two tours in Afghanistan. And she's also a ninja. So you guys might want to watch your step."

Lena met his gaze, her blue eyes dancing with laughter.

"Whoa," Peyton said. "I didn't know the army trained you to be a ninja."

Before Chad could tell Peyton to take his stoned ass away from their table, the larger of the two guys crossed behind Lena, moving fast for an impaired man. He swung one leg over the bench and sat down. Too close, dammit.

Lena's eyes widened, her hand tightening around the cone until it snapped in her hand, covering her fingers in ice cream.

"Back away from my girl." Chad was on his feet, his cone tossed to the ground. He planted his palms on the table, ready to physically remove Peyton from the table. This was no longer a game. He could see the panic in Lena's wild-eyed expression.

"She's a ninja, man," Peyton said. "I need to talk to her."

Hero abandoned his place in the grass, racing toward his owner. He gave two sharp warning barks at the confused, high-off-his-ass idiot.

"I was joking about being a ninja, but she did serve. And fast movements startle her, OK?" Chad said, his voice low and even.

Hero placed his front paws on the bench, wedging his body between Lena's trembling limbs and Peyton's larger frame. Getting the message, Peyton stood and stepped away from the picnic table. A second later and Chad would have physically removed him.

"Sorry man," Peyton said, his brow furrowed, his gaze fixed on the angry retriever. "We got in the mood for pizza on the way over, you know? And I've always wanted to meet a real ninja."

"Not today," Chad said. "You might want to order your pizza. Now."

Chad waited until they walked away before sitting down. "Lena, I'm sorry—" He caught himself. Those weren't the words she needed to hear. She didn't need pity, not from him or anyone else.

"—about your ice cream," he added.

She picked up a napkin and started cleaning her hands. "Me too," she said, her voice shaky.

Chad glanced at the stoned men stumbling through the door to the restaurant, wondering if he should go after them and throw a few punches after all. After robbing Lena of her teasing, confident tone, Tim and Peyton deserved to have their butts kicked.

"I'd only had one good lick of the vanilla," she continued, the tremble in her tone fading with each word. "I was thinking about moving on to the chocolate. You know, spice things up a little bit."

Relief swept over him. If she'd been anyone else, he would have pulled her close, held her tight, and told how much he admired the way she refused to let her fears hold her captive.

"Lena, I'm ready to move past vanilla whenever you are. With you, I'm up for anything."

Lena followed Chad to his truck, forcing a calm she didn't feel. Hero clung to her side, his body pressed against her leg as they walked. Children and stoned men who believed in ninjas—those things didn't send normal people diving headfirst into a panic attack.

She stopped by the passenger side door and rested her forehead against the window, closing her eyes. "Shit," she murmured. "*Shit.* I just wanted to eat a pizza with my pretend boyfriend."

"Hey now," Chad said. "I'm not complaining."

She opened her eyes and turned her head, spotting Chad leaning against the rear of his truck. He wouldn't approach her with her eyes closed, she realized.

"You have good ears," she said.

He headed toward her, walking around to open her door. "I grew up with two brothers and a sister. I think they would tell you I have selective hearing. Before we finalized the sale with Moore Timber, I would run the other way when I heard the word 'paperwork.' Hop in, Lena."

She climbed into the truck, buckling her belt as Hero claimed the space between them. Chad pulled out of the lot, waving to the growing crowd at the picnic tables.

"So you're continuing the job search tomorrow?" he asked as they turned onto the two-lane country road leading to the Summers family home.

"Yes." She needed to find something soon or she'd be forced to turn to either her ex or her parents for money. Neither option appealed to her. She didn't want to give them one more reason to look at her and see failure. "Is there an Internet café in town? I need to find a computer."

"Come by the house in the morning," Chad said. "Katie has a desktop in the study that you can use."

"I don't want to be in the way." *Or face an inquisition*, she thought.

"You won't be." Chad steered the truck down the bumpy driveway. "You can help yourself to the fridge. There will be coffee. Brody makes a pot every morning. And Hero's welcome."

"You had me at coffee," she said. "Thank you."

He parked the truck by the barn, but kept the engine running as he turned to her. Flashing his panty-melting smile. "You're my girl, now."

"It's not real, Chad," she murmured. The parts of her body that would have ignored that smile twenty-four hours ago sparked with interest. Now that she knew his smiles weren't empty promises.

"Lena, we made it real tonight. After what happened—"

"I'm sorry," she said. The words felt like a reflex.

"No, Lena. Don't apologize." His smile faded. "Word will get back to Eric that we went out for pizza, and I just about murdered one of his guys for sitting down next to you."

"Eric knows I struggle with strangers approaching me," she said softly.

"Yeah, and he knows I'm not the guy who stands up and plays hero. That's not me, Lena."

No, it wasn't. Chad charmed everyone, men and women, with his looks and his words. He wasn't the big, bad alpha man rushing in to save the day. No one felt threatened by him. Until tonight. The way he'd stared down the man who honest-to-God thought she was a ninja—pure alpha male. And she had a feeling it wasn't an act.

"Sometimes we surprise ourselves," she said. *And prove we're not who we thought we were.*

Hope blossomed. Maybe she had it in her too. Maybe she'd prove to the people who'd written her off as broken that she could glue the pieces back together.

"Yeah, I guess we do." His brown eyes studied her, brooding and intense. His jaw tightened, his gaze dropping to her lips. His fingers gripped the steering wheel as if he had to hold on to something to keep from reaching for her.

Desire—spurred by the knowledge that this man didn't expect any more than she could give—took over. She opened the passenger side door, but didn't move to get out. As soon as Hero jumped down, she closed it and turned back to Chad.

She focused on his lips, unable to look away. If she kissed him, that empty feeling might return. Right now, she felt a rush of emotions when she was with Chad. He put her at ease and made her laugh.

"Lena?"

She raised one hand, pressing a finger to his lips. Moving her hand to his cheek, she leaned forward until her mouth hovered close to his. She wanted this kiss even if tomorrow she freaked out at the thought of touching her lips to his. Even if it left her wishing she could run and hide, or that horrible numb feeling she'd endured for so many months returned and she shunned everyone again, she wanted to take the leap.

Closing her eyes, she brushed her lips over his—a soft touch, nothing more. But this kiss—it didn't feel meaningless. Her heart raced, but it wasn't headed for panic central. The blood flowing through her didn't freeze. Just the opposite. Every part of her burned with desire for more.

She kissed him again, opening her mouth to his, deepening the connection. And he didn't back down. His lips moved over hers, vying for control, letting her feel his desire, his need—it was potent and demanding, a perfect match for the wild lust pulsing through her.

Maybe they could take this further, making love here, in his truck . . .

Uncertainty rose up, and she felt her breathing change. The panic she'd fought at the pizza place had receded, but it hadn't disappeared. She could feel it waiting on the sidelines.

Chad drew back, breaking the kiss as if he understood that they'd reached an imaginary tipping point. Staring into her eyes, his lips curved into his devilish smile. "Why don't you head in, Lena?"

"You're not coming?"

He let out a short, rough laugh. "No, beautiful. Not tonight. But I left your present on your nightstand in case you want to."

I don't want the toy. I want you. But her mind knew better. Tonight wasn't the night to push her boundaries. Not when she was inching her way toward normal.

"I've had enough excitement for one night," he added. "I'll keep the headlights on so you can get inside. And I'll see you at the house in the morning."

She nodded as she opened the door and climbed down from his truck.

"And Lena?"

She glanced over her shoulder, her dog pressing against her side the minute her feet touched the ground.

"Dream of me."

Chapter 9

CHAD LEANED HIS head back against the tiles, the water rushing over him. Daylight poured in the small tempered glass window. Eyes closed, his mind revisited last night, in the studio, before pizza. The way her hands moved over her breasts, the soft, needy sounds she'd made, her pleas for more—

"Chad! Where are you? I swear, when I find you . . ."

A familiar female voice echoed in the hall, stealing him away from the fantasy. The door swung open, the brass knob hitting the tiled wall. The wimpy hook Brody had installed to give them the illusion of privacy proved to be no match for the ranting, raving woman who'd invaded the bathroom.

"Is it true?" Katie demanded.

Chad pulled back the curtain just enough to show his face, careful to keep the rest of his body hidden behind the hunter green fabric. It was a damn good thing his sister hadn't chosen one of those clear plastic shower curtains.

"Kinda naked here," he said.

Her eyes narrowed, her wild red curls surrounding her face like a pile of Medusa's snakes. Yeah, she was sure as hell pissed off, and he had a hunch he knew why. Somebody had spread the word about his "date."

"Did you take Lena out?" Katie demanded, folding her arms in front of her chest.

More footsteps sounded in the hall. Chad had a sinking feeling the number of people in his bathroom was about to double. Liam Trulane, the number two at Moore Timber and his kid sister's boyfriend, poked his head in the bathroom, spotted Chad, and quickly retreated.

"Katie," Liam called from the hall. "Let him finish his shower first."

"No," she snapped.

"Great, now I have an audience," he said, pulling the curtain closed and stepping back under the water to rinse his hair.

"I'm leaving, man," Liam said.

"Can't you toss her over your shoulder and take her with you?" Chad called.

"Your sister?" Liam let out a laugh. "Not if I want to see tomorrow."

"Did you take Lena out on a date?" Katie repeated.

His hair rinsed, Chad turned off the water and stuck his hand out. "Hand me a towel, will you?"

She slapped a towel into his hand. "Trish from the pizza place told Georgia that you nearly took Peyton

Monroe's head off for sitting next to her. Why would you take her out? You've seen her dog and the way she reacts when anyone gets near her."

"I thought she'd like to split a pizza. Talk and get to know each other better." Chad dried off. Wrapping the towel around his waist, he drew back the curtain. "Peyton and Tim showed up stoned and got a little too close. It spooked her, so I told them to back the hell off."

"Hey, who called a family meeting and forgot to invite me?" Brody, the oldest of the four Summers siblings, leaned against the bathroom door frame, his arms folded to match Katie's what-did-you-do-now-Chad look.

"Chad took Lena on a date after I invited her to stay in the apartment," Katie said.

Brow furrowed, Brody's attention darted back and forth between them. "Lena, the woman with the dog? Georgia's friend?"

"Same one," Katie said. "The dog helps with her PTSD and the fact that she doesn't like to be touched or let people close. How's that working out for you, Chad?"

Pretty damn good considering that kiss last night. Sure, he'd given her one helluva orgasm before dinner, but that kiss had blown him away. But it wasn't his place to kiss and tell.

"None of your fucking business, Katie." Chad stepped out of the tub. "I left you alone to make your own decisions when it came to Liam, right? Because you're a big girl. Well, I'm bigger and older than you, so leave me the hell alone."

"But—"

He stared down at his sister. "And don't you dare write Lena off. She's fighting her way back from something you and I can't begin to understand. The only thing we can do is grant her the space and the respect she deserves. And if she wants to join me for dinner, well, that's her call."

"I'm not giving up on her," Katie said stubbornly. "I'm looking out for her. The last thing she *deserves* is to fall for you."

"You know, sis, some people find me charming."

"You are charming. And sweet when you want to be." She raised her hand, poking him in the chest. "But if you hurt her—"

"I won't." Chad dropped his voice low. "Not that it concerns either of you, but I like her."

"Katie, he's right," Brody said. "This isn't your call."

"I hate to interrupt." Liam appeared in the doorway again. "But Lena's here. In the kitchen. I offered her coffee and she asked about using the computer."

Chad nodded. "I told her she could use the study. She needs to get online and the library is closed today. That won't be a problem, will it?"

Katie gave him one last searching look. "No. I'll get her set up."

"When you're done," Brody said, shifting his gaze between Katie and Chad, "and when you're dressed, we need to talk. About Josh. There's been no change and we need to start making some decisions."

Chad nodded. "I'll find you in the kitchen."

The bathroom door closed, leaving him alone with the realization that he meant those words. *I like her*. Their relationship might be a fraud, but he liked Lena. And he'd just locked them into this lie. It was too late to turn back now and tell the town, his family, and Eric Moore that it was a sham. Now they had to move forward with it, or stage a breakup. Either way, people would talk.

Chad rested his hands on the vanity and stared into the mirror. "I sure as hell better live up to my end of the bargain."

AN HOUR LATER, Chad sat on the edge of his younger brother's hospital bed, wishing he could take a quick ride in his helicopter. He needed to clear his head, not dive into what promised to be the first of many serious conversations for the day. And he refused to skirt the second one. When he got back to the house, he wanted to talk to Lena and learn more about what she'd seen and done while serving her country.

As much as he hated to admit it, Katie had a point. He couldn't hurt her. And to avoid going down that road, he needed to know if he could fulfill his side of their deal without pushing too far too fast. Sure, she could always say no, but that might not be enough depending on what had happened overseas.

"Chad? What the hell, man? You look grim," Josh said, sitting up in his hospital bed. Not much older than their little sister, Josh had the same red hair, green eyes, and pale skin. Chad and Brody had inherited their father's brown hair and eyes, their skin not quite so pale. Although Chad suspected his baby brother's paleness was due to the weeks spent lying in a hospital bed.

Josh had traded in his hospital gown for sweats and T-shirt after waking from his coma, but he still wore the big white bandage around his head—a clear and present reminder that he belonged here. The other reasons, the ones not visible, those were the ones they needed to talk about today.

"Did one of the nurses turn you down?" Josh added.

"He's off the market," Brody said from the chair beside the bed. "He's dating someone."

Josh's red eyebrows shot up. "Chad? No shit. I thought you kept it casual. Never more than one night, afraid that every woman you date will walk out on you just like Mom abandoned Dad."

The words stung. More than Chad wanted to admit. "You can't remember what you had for breakfast or how the hell you landed in the hospital, but you want to play Oprah when it comes to my love life?"

Josh shrugged. "Short-term memory loss, bro. I remember the things that matter."

"I don't think who is in my bed should make that list. And for the record, I don't steer clear of relationships because Mom left." *Not entirely.* "I just like women too much to settle down."

He heard Brody shift in his chair and knew his brother was thinking back to this morning's conversation in the bathroom.

"But Lena's special," Chad added.

"Lena? The girl with the dog who moved into Eric's place? I heard from some guys on the crew I was working with before I ended up here that she doesn't like to be touched. Not even a handshake. How the hell does that work?" Josh leaned forward as he delivered his rapid-fire questions.

"If you think I'm giving you a play-by-play—"

"Enough," Brody said. He rose and began to pace. "We didn't come here to talk about what Chad is doing at night."

Josh leaned back against the pile of hospital pillows. "Why are you here?"

Pausing at the foot of the bed, Brody hovered over them, looking every inch the big brother who'd carried the freaking weight of the family on his shoulders since their dad passed away seven years ago. It didn't matter that his siblings were technically adults, even Katie, who'd been eighteen at the time. By a matter of weeks, but still, legal. Brody had taken over the struggling family business. He'd made sure there was food on the table and a roof over their heads. Now here he was again, taking charge. And Chad didn't begrudge him this role at all.

"We've talked," Brody began. "And Katie would be here too, but she got a call about a hog that needed a new home."

"I get laid up and we become pig farmers?" Josh joked. But the words failed to mask the quiver in his voice.

Chad rested his hand on his little brother's leg. It must be hell to wake up in a strange place every day, unsure why you were there. "Katie and Liam are starting a pig farm," he said. "Or at least adding hogs to their barn of rescued misfits."

"Katie's with Liam Trulane?" Josh said, and Chad wanted to kick his own ass square into the next county. The last thing his brother knew, Katie had walked away from Liam. Sure, she'd explained everything to Josh, telling him about her wild love affair and the fact that she planned to move in with the man she once despised. But even if she'd told him yesterday, chances were he wouldn't remember today. It was as if his memory drew a firm line between before and after the accident.

"Yes," Brody said in his I'm-taking-charge-now voice. "She is. And Chad's right. The pigs are their problem. But we talked with her this morning after I learned that the hospital plans to release you. They want to send you to a long-term care center by the university."

"I can't go home?" Josh asked, his eyes darting between his big brothers. Chad felt like an ass looking away, but knew it was better if their oldest brother, their ringleader since grade school, handled this one.

Brody shook his head. "Not yet. They claim the doctors there have some experience with short-term memory loss following a traumatic brain injury."

"So you think it's the right move?" Josh said slowly. Chad tightened his grip on his brother's leg. At twenty-seven, his little brother looked like a lost child, and it freaking gutted him.

"It's not our only move," Chad said.

Brody nodded. "We'll be interviewing specialists from all over the country. New York, Chicago, Dallas, I have a list of the top doctors who have experience helping people who have suffered similar injuries."

"What about the business?" Josh asked. "You've got a company to run."

Chad looked at Brody, saw the pained expression on his big brother's face, and decided to take this one. "We sold the trucking company to Moore Timber," Chad said. "We closed on the deal. You're a rich man now. And we've got the free time to make the calls. Just sit back and relax. Enjoy having the pretty nurses fawn over you."

Josh nodded, but Chad had a feeling his kid brother didn't remember the sale. He'd known it was in the works. And Josh had been on board with the decision, pushing for it even, but it had still been up in the air at the time of the accident.

"We're going to keep you in the loop," Brody promised. "Even if we have to tell you the same things over and over. And we're going to find a way to get you back to normal."

Chad nodded in agreement, but his thoughts drifted to Lena and her fierce determination to travel the same road. He'd do whatever it took to help them. But normal? The past forty-eight hours had shown him that it wasn't an easy place to find.

Chapter 10

TURNING AWAY FROM the computer screen, Lena picked up the envelope she'd carried over from the apartment this morning and promptly abandoned beside her lukewarm coffee. The Summers family had left her alone all day. Chad had poked his head in once to tell her that he needed to swing by the hospital, but otherwise, silence. She'd used the time, and the high-speed connection, to send out a dozen résumés to prospective employers in the area, everything from night security to receptionist. But now she needed to read the packet of papers Malcolm had dropped off yesterday.

Sliding the cover letter out, she scanned the paragraphs. The words formed a tangled mess in her mind. A Silver Star. The vice president. Lena set the paper down and rested her forehead on it. Her constant companion—who might or might not be invited to the ceremony—moved at her feet, pressing close against her leg.

Would she be ready in one month to stand up in front of the vice president, her family, and the press? She'd come so far in the past few months, in large part due to Hero. But she hadn't pushed. She'd given herself the time and space to heal, removing the people in her life who demanded results. The ones who'd been there when she'd hit her lowest point, afraid to sleep due to nightmares, terrified to leave the house, or let even her husband close to her. She'd crawled her way back from that point, bit by bit, on her own. Still, the ceremony might be too much too soon.

"If you need a nap, there is a sofa."

She lifted her head and spotted Chad standing in the doorway, holding a plate and a glass. "You're back. How did it go at the hospital?"

"All right." His smile faltered and she wondered if there was more to it. "I can confirm that news of our relationship is spreading. Even Josh knows. And I don't think he's going to forget anytime soon. The nurses were gossiping like schoolgirls when I walked past. They'll make it part of their job to remind him."

"That's good, right?"

Chad nodded, moving into the study. "Yeah, it's good. But I'm not sure Katie sees it that way."

"I'll talk to her," Lena said, though she had to admit that she liked having a friend who would stand up for her.

"I made you a late lunch." Chad set a turkey sandwich on the desk, and the glass of water. "We were out of jelly, so no PB&J today. But that's the real thing. No soy."

"Thanks, I've been sending out résumés and forgot to take a break."

"Is that what you're working on now?" he asked.

"No." She handed him the official letter. "I need to let them know if I'm going to the ceremony."

He scanned the paper. "It's at the army base south of here? That's not far. Only a day's drive."

"I know," she said, turning back to the computer, checking her e-mail more to keep her hands busy than because she expected a response on a Sunday afternoon. "I'm not worried about getting there. I don't mind traveling."

Still holding the letter, he settled into a chair across from the desk. "What does bother you?"

Lena took a deep breath and turned the swivel chair to face him. "You mean aside from attractive men climbing in my bed? Or strangers getting too close when they think I'm a ninja?"

He nodded. "You can tell me to shut up if you want, but I'd like to know what happened over there. You said it was your dad's dream for you to go to West Point and join the army. But what happened when you got there?"

"Nothing."

Chad raised an eyebrow. "They don't award Silver Stars for sitting on your hands in a war zone. I looked it up. It's the third highest honor. And nothing doesn't lead to . . ."

"Post-traumatic stress disorder?"

"Yeah."

"There wasn't a single event that I can point to and say that's the moment everything unraveled," she said. "I was deployed twice, and both times I worked alongside my team. I did my job."

"What did you do?"

"I was an intelligence officer. Surveillance, reconnaissance, advice, that sort of thing."

Chad let out a low whistle. "That's pretty impressive."

"There were a lot of impressive men and women over there," she said. "I just happened to be in the right place at the right time toward the end of my second tour. We came under attack from insurgents, and I ran back and forth from the TOC, that's the tactical operations center, while under fire, relaying the necessary information."

"And what?" he prompted.

"I carried the injured out, using my body as a shield," she said. "They all made it home alive. Every single one of them."

"Wow." Chad leaned forward in his chair, resting his forearms on his thighs.

"I know I did a great job out there," she added. "And that's the reason I'm getting a medal. But—"

"How many lives did you save?"

"That day? Seven."

"And you didn't get hit?"

"You know how in the movies the good guy runs through a stream of bullets, never getting shot? It was like that. I had a team of guys covering me and I returned fire, but still, I felt invincible."

Her smile faded, her gaze dropping to the untouched sandwich. "And then I served the remaining months of my tour, came home, and . . . and I fell apart. It started with nightmares. About that day. And others. I couldn't sleep. I felt like I always had to keep watch. And that hypervigilance infiltrated the rest of my life. It got worse, and I didn't want to leave the house.

"I know I'm one of the lucky ones," she continued. "I'm learning to cope. It's just not going to happen overnight, or in the next few weeks. I keep pushing my limits. But sometimes they push back."

"Take all the time you need, Lena." He smiled, soft and gentle.

"Thank you." She wondered if he understood how much those words meant to her. She'd spent months surrounded by friends and family who wanted to make it better, to find the cure-all, whether it was a complicated drug cocktail or more time in therapy. They wanted to close the book on the terrors that followed her around.

"Can I take you out tonight?" he asked. "I was thinking Italian. Or maybe Mexican since we had pizza last night? If you want, we could grab take-out and eat here."

"I can't. I promised Georgia I'd stop by for dinner. Before we made our deal." She drew her lower lip between her teeth, thinking about what she'd be missing before, or maybe after, their "date." "I could cancel."

"No, I'll buy you dinner tomorrow. And tonight, I'll be waiting when you get home," he said, but this time he didn't offer his I'll-charm-your-panties-off smile. His intense brown eyes were hot and wanting. "If you want to challenge the boundaries, hell, I'm right there with you. I want you, Lena. But the rules stand."

"No guns," she said. "In bed."

"And we stop whenever you want. Don't forget that." Chad stood. "Will you do one thing for me?"

She nodded, expecting the next words out his mouth to be dirty and wild. *Have your pink toy ready. Take your panties off before you come upstairs tonight.*

"Call whomever you need to call and tell you'd like to accept the medal," he said. "You can always cancel. But you earned this honor. And I hate to see fear hold you back from accepting it."

"I might run as soon as I reach the stage," she said.

"I'll come with you, grab the medal, and follow you to the truck," he said. "Look, I know you're searching for normal, to be who you were before. But Lena, I don't think there is anything wrong with who you are now."

Her heart rate kicked up a notch as he turned and headed for the door. And this time it had nothing to do with panic. She'd wanted to hear those words ever since she'd returned home and realized she couldn't slip into civilian life like a pair of old shoes. But she hadn't expected them to come from him—the man who occupied only a temporary place in her life.

THE FRONT DOOR to Eric and Georgia's sprawling timber frame home opened a crack and the smell of melted chocolate drifted out. Cookies. Knowing Georgia, they were probably made from scratch, contained beet juice to make them "healthy," and had enough chewy, high-calorie goodness that Lena wouldn't care about the tablespoon of vegetables.

"You can come in, but Hero has to stay out there," a small, commanding voice said. She glanced down and saw Nate, Eric's three-soon-to-be-four-year-old nephew holding the door, a stuffed green dinosaur with a big toothy smile tucked under his arm.

"I need my dog with me, Nate. He's my superhero, remember?" she said, borrowing the words Georgia had used to explain Hero's presence in their home when Lena first moved in to stay with them.

"He'll eat my T-rex," Nate said. "He chewed my big, big bridge the last time you were here."

Hero glanced up at her, his lips forming a doggie smile around his chew toy. The expression on his canine face said, *I'm so guilty.*

Turning away from Hero, she crouched down to the little boy's level, trying to think of a reason that would convince the child to let the guilty-as-charged Hero in the door.

"I'm sorry about the bridge. I promise to replace it." It was on her list of things to buy as soon as she had a job, right below new cell phone. "If he promises to behave, can we come in?"

"No."

"Nate?" Georgia's voice echoed in the great room just beyond the front door. "Nate, is Lena at the door?"

"Yes, but she can't come in with the dog."

Georgia appeared, wearing an "I Heart Oregon" apron over her jeans and T-shirt. "Kiddo, Lena needs Hero. He fights the bears for her."

Nate studied the dog for a moment and then nodded,

opening the door wide. "But he can't come near my toys."

"Deal," Lena said, wrapping her hand around Hero's collar as she led him into the house. Holding the stuffed duck between his teeth, Hero glanced longingly at the wooden train tracks. But she drew him away, following Georgia into the kitchen. Through the open doorway, they could see Nate playing with his toys.

"You know," Lena said, releasing the dog, "I don't think Hero would win a battle with a bear."

"Not a real bear." Georgia opened the oven and withdrew a cookie sheet. The smell of fresh-baked chocolate chips filled the room. "It's how he refers to his nightmares. And mine."

"Oh." The ever-present image of battered, bloody bodies moved to the forefront of her mind. Panic followed close behind, running hand in hand with the feeling she would never be safe. In the other room, a crash echoed, and Lena jumped.

Hero abandoned his chew toy on the floor and nudged her thigh. She glanced down at the dog, his head cocked to one side, his friendly eyes studying her as if to say: *So we're doing this right now? Freaking out? Over a kid dropping his toy trains?*

No. She focused on Hero. Mouth open, tongue hanging out, doggie smile in place—watching him, she pushed the memories into hibernation. Spring could come at any moment waking her slumbering "bears," but she could face them now.

"Maybe Hero would win," Lena said.

"Of course he will." Georgia smiled and nodded to the kitchen table. "I fed Nate earlier, and our dinner is on the stove. But we can sample the dessert first if you want."

"I always want dessert first."

"I figured you might, seeing as you lost your ice cream cone last night. I heard all about it." Georgia piled cookies onto a plate and turned to the fridge. "Milk?"

"Actually, tonight I'd like a glass of wine."

"And I was hoping you'd say that." Georgia opened the fridge and pulled out a bottle of white wine. "After a glass or two, maybe you'll spill the details of your date with Chad Summers."

"You heard." Lena accepted the drink, raising the glass to her lips.

"I ran into Ariel at the grocery store. She heard from Trish, who told everyone who would listen in church this morning." Georgia piled a plate with cookies and sat down at the head of the table, her gaze darting to the child in the other room making dinosaur noises.

"On the trail yesterday you said he was the perfect gentleman when he found you in bed," Georgia continued. "But you didn't mention a date."

"He asked me yesterday afternoon. It was just pizza."

"Hmm, I don't think it is ever 'just pizza' with Chad."

"I like him," Lena said, knowing she couldn't tell her friend about their arrangement. If she told Georgia, Eric would find out and ruin their plan. "But while we were out, one of the guys, someone who works for Eric, got too close and I panicked."

"I'm sorry," Georgia murmured, her smile fading.

Lena shrugged. "It happens. But not once did Chad look at me like it was my fault, or suggest that I was being irrational. He didn't ask how do we fix this? How do we make sure this doesn't happen again?"

"I'd kick his ass if he did," Georgia said. "So would Katie."

"It's nice to be with someone who accepts my boundaries," Lena said, borrowing Chad's word. "He's not trying to change me or fix me."

Probably because we aren't really dating, she thought. *He isn't looking at the long-term picture.*

Lena bit into a cookie. "These are good. Did you skip the beet juice?"

"I'm learning to hide it better," Georgia said. "But before we change the subject, I need to do my part as your friend and warn you, Chad has a reputation—"

"So do I," Lena cut in. *The woman who couldn't be touched, the one who crumbled like the cookie in her hand.* "He looked past that. I think I can do the same for him."

And she hoped that the rest of the town, Eric Moore and the others involved with getting Chad back up in the air, flying his helicopter over the forest, would too. Maybe not right away . . .

The kitchen timer beeped and Georgia jumped up. "That's dinner. Eric should be home any minute to put Nate to bed. Then we can eat and you can tell me more."

"Nothing more to tell."

"I'm not pushing you to kiss and tell." Georgia moved to the stove, lifting the lid of a large pot. "Unless there is something you want to share?"

He writes notes filled with wicked promises...

"There's one thing." Lena picked up a second cookie. "You make the best chocolate chip cookies."

AN HOUR LATER, while Georgia went to say good night to Nate for the third time after Eric's very last story, Lena borrowed their landline and dialed Chad's cell. The glass and a half of wine had left her feeling bold, brazen, and too tipsy to drive.

"Hello, Chad here," a familiar, easygoing voice announced after the second ring.

"I need you." Lena closed her eyes. *Wrong words!* One glass of wine made her an idiot.

"Lena? Is everything all right?" Chad demanded. "Are you at Georgia and Eric's?"

"Yes," she said. "And I was hoping you could pick me up. I've been drinking."

"I'll be right over."

Setting the phone down, she reached for a notepad and pen. She'd failed to deliver bold and brazen on the phone, but when he arrived, she'd make it clear that tonight was not going to end with her alone in bed with a toy.

Chapter 11

CHAD PARKED IN front of Eric Moore's house armed with a bottle of water. He'd been waiting for her call, hopeful that Lena would give him the chance to prove he could live up to his end of their deal. But he'd kind of been hoping she'd say something like *I want you to kiss me until I come against your mouth*, not *I'm too tipsy to drive.*

Climbing down from his truck, he spotted Hero first, then Lena. Georgia stood in the doorway waving to him while her fiancé followed Lena to the truck.

"Thanks for getting her home safe," Georgia called.

"Anytime." He waved to Georgia before turning his attention to Lena and her escort. "Hey Eric, I'll see you at the office tomorrow?"

Eric nodded, stopping ten feet away from Lena and the truck. "Yes. But before you go, can I have a word?"

"Sure." He glanced at Lena, confirmed that she wasn't

falling down drunk, and headed over to his boss/business partner. "But make it quick."

"I wanted to let you know that I fired Tim today," Eric said. "He showed up and one of the guys suspected he was under the influence. After hearing the gossip about your run-in with him the other night, I decided to let him go. But he left with plenty of hard feelings, and not all of them were aimed at me. Hell, he seemed downright unstable when he stormed out of the office. Next time you run into him, I have a feeling he'll have a few things to get off his chest."

"Sorry it went down like that," Chad said, relieved that Eric hadn't marched across his front yard to demand Chad keep his hands off Lena. "But thanks for the heads-up."

Eric slapped him on the shoulder. "Have a good night."

"Planning on it." Chad turned his attention to Lena as his boss headed for his fiancée. He'd expected a waddling, drunken mess, but no, she appeared calm and composed, her steps measured and deliberate.

"How much did you drink?" he demanded.

"One glass," she said, climbing into the passenger seat. "Before dinner. Maybe another half glass after. Enough to know I should come back for my truck in the morning. Georgia promised to pick me up after she takes Nate to preschool."

He held out the water. "I'm not sure you'll need this, Miss One-and-a-Half Glasses, but just in case."

Lena took the bottle with one hand and held out a crumpled piece of paper with the other. "For you."

He glanced at the oddly folded Post-it. "Origami?"

"It's what I meant to say on the phone."

Chad unfolded the paper and scanned the neatly printed words.

I think I need further instructions. While I'm on my knees.

"That's why you called?" His voice was hoarse as he tried to focus on the here and now, not the fact that he wanted to start giving orders in his boss's front yard.

"I was feeling wild. And maybe a little brazen."

"Lena." If she kept talking, he might say to hell with the fact that Eric Moore owned this house.

"I think you should start the truck now," she said.

Chad nodded, walking around to the driver's side, his mind filled with the images of Lena naked and kneeling. But shit, she might throw the brakes on when they got to that point.

"Are you sure about this?" He put the truck in gear and steered it down the drive to the main road.

"Yes. But I have to warn you. It has been a while since I took orders. It might take some practice."

His mouth went dry. Words escaped him. He always had the right ones on the tip of his tongue, but Lena left him speechless, and sporting a hard-on that begged him to pull over and let her *practice* until sunrise.

"I might need to a give a few commands of my own," she continued, her tone matter-of-fact, as if discussing what she had for dinner. "What I have in mind, it's on the edge of vanilla."

Chad pressed on the brakes, coming to an abrupt halt at the red traffic signal. "Lena, I need you to do me a favor. Sit quietly and drink your water. Not another word until we get home. Can you do that for me?"

"Yes, sir," she murmured.

His cock jumped at the potent combination of the word "sir" and her teasing tone. And then she smiled, her face lit with sensual promise. That gleam in her blue eyes—how could a man see that and walk away from her? He had a feeling it would be burned into his memory. Hell, he might wait damn near forever to see it again.

His hands tightened around the wheel and his jaw clenched as he turned his attention back to the road. The streets were quiet, even for a Sunday night. If they'd hit traffic, he might have been tempted to break a few laws to get her home and into the studio apartment.

"You're sure you haven't had too much to drink? And yes, you can answer that."

"I'm not drunk, Chad. I know what I'm doing, what I'm asking for," she said, her hands holding tight to the plastic water bottle. "Worried I'll stop you once you start giving the orders?"

He turned down his drive and sped toward home. Parking beside the barn, he faced her. "You can always stop me. Understand?"

"Yes, sir."

He caught another glimpse of that sexy glimmer in her

eyes before she opened the truck door and stepped down. Struggling with his seat belt, Chad raced to catch up. He followed her inside and up the stairs, careful to give her space when he wanted to pull her close and freaking *take* her.

Inside the small studio, Lena led the reluctant golden retriever to the bathroom and closed the door. She turned around, her hands on her hips as she studied the wooden chairs by the two-person table, and judging from her gaze, found them lacking.

"Put your arms up like this," she said, placing her hands behind her head.

"OK." He obeyed, interlacing his fingers at the base of his neck. "But I thought I was giving the orders."

"We're not there yet," she murmured. She lowered her arms and walked toward him, her blue eyes shining with determination.

Her fingers brushed his belt buckle. Working the leather free, she unbuttoned his pants. Her hand touched his skin and he groaned. Chad kept his eyes trained on her as she hooked her thumbs in his jeans and drew them down.

"There are Christmas trees and elves on your underwear," she said without looking up.

"I was feeling festive this morning."

Her fingers slipped beneath the elastic band. "Have you been a good boy?"

"That depends."

Her hands moved to his low back, drawing his boxers down over his ass, her palms gliding across his skin. If she took one step closer, her body would be pressed against him. *One step.*

"Will I be rewarded for good behavior?" he asked.

"Maybe. But if you were bad . . ."

Her blue eyes widened as she stared at his cock. She'd abandoned project Remove His Boxers at his thighs, but he wasn't complaining.

"This morning, I drank the last of the milk and put the carton back in the fridge," he said. "Does that count?"

"Yes." She stepped back. "I might have to tie you up."

"I understand."

She reached for his pants, pulling his belt free from the loops. Then she disappeared from view. He heard her moving behind him, then felt the leather strap wrap around his wrist. She maneuvered his belt, her hands moving quickly as if she knew what she was doing. The buckle tightened, binding his wrists together behind his head.

"Too tight?" she said softly.

"No," he said, not giving a damn if it cut off the circulation to his hands. Right now, the blood in his body was rushing south. "Move in front me, Lena. I need to see you."

She obeyed, standing so close he could have reached out and touched her—if his hands weren't tied. Searching her gorgeous face, he tried to find a hint of panic, a sign she wasn't ready for this—and came up empty.

Halle—freaking—lujah.

"I'm ready, Chad." She lowered to her knees, brushed her long, blond hair over her shoulders as she looked up at him. "Tell me what you want."

"Start at the bottom and work your way to the top."

Eyes closed, her arms at her sides, she pressed her tongue to the base of his cock. He groaned as she licked her way to the tip.

"And now?" she asked, her lips hovering over the head. He fought the urge to thrust his hips.

"Wrap your mouth around me, beautiful."

Lena followed his orders and his hips flexed as if the muscles had disconnected from his brain.

"That's it. Take me deep."

Her lips ran down his hard length, her tongue swirling.

"Put your hand around me," he demanded, the words escaping before he stopped to think that maybe she wouldn't feel comfortable touching him. Maybe that was too much. But she followed his orders, wrapping her fingers around him, stroking him up and down as her mouth worked its sweet magic.

His mind blanked, his hips thrusting into her. Eyes closed, he pressed his head back against his bound hands. Low moans and a chorus of "Fuck yes" and "oh Lena" replaced commands until he exploded.

He was a bastard for not giving her a moment's warning. And he'd feel like shit about that in a minute. But right now? With his dick buried in her mouth, his body rocked from head to toe with mind-blowing pleasure, he felt as if he'd been rocketed to freaking heaven.

Slowly, the orgasm faded. He opened his eyes as she released him. Her gaze met his, her blue eyes shining with an I-know-I-rocked-your-world look.

"I'm sorry," he said. "I got a little carried away."

She let out a soft laugh. "Chad, you can play the gentleman when we're out. But not in here with me."

"All right. I'm not sorry. Untie me and I'll show you that I'm feeling pretty damn grateful."

She stepped back, her smile faded. "I don't think—"

"I won't touch you, Lena. Not if you don't want me to. The rules are still the rules. But if you think I'm going to leave you alone with your toy . . ." He nodded to the gift bag sitting on her nightstand. He had a hunch the vibrator was inside.

His hands pulled at the belt. "Untie me, Lena."

She shook her head, and he saw a hint of the wicked, wanton gleam in her eyes.

"Lena."

Her fingers gathered the fabric of her long, flowing skirt. Then, in one swift motion, she pulled her dress over her head and tossed it aside. Her bra followed.

"Chad?"

"Yes," he murmured, staring at her full breasts. "I'm listening. And I swear, I'd look at your lips if I could, but right now I can't stop thinking about running my teeth over your nipples."

Her hands moved to her breasts, testing the full weight, pinching her nipples between her thumb and finger.

"Chad, do you like to watch?" Her hands traveled south to her hips, drawing her panties down her long legs. She stepped out, her underwear joining her dress.

Chad looked up at her face. "Lena, if it turns you on I'm game. I'm dying to touch you, taste you, but if you want me to watch, I will."

She moved to the edge of the bed and sat. Leaning back, she spread her thighs wide, running one hand over the places he'd explored with the vibrator.

"Come closer," she said, the words more command than invitation.

His fingers ached to touch her, but he couldn't. With his hands still bound behind his head, Chad fell to his knees at her feet. If he leaned forward, he could replace her fingers with his tongue. But he didn't want to stop there. He wanted to kiss his way up her body to her lips before making his way back down.

"Lena," he murmured.

She lifted her hips up to meet his lips. "Make me scream, Chad. I want to say your name as I come."

SHE WATCHED, UNABLE to look away as his lips touched her. His tongue brushed back and forth over her, teasing her clit. Slipping lower, he drew circles around her entrance, taunting her, before moving up, varying the pressure and rhythm in a wicked dance designed to drive her wild.

Then he stopped, damn him. And she whimpered, a foreign sound on the edge of begging.

"Say my name, Lena," he growled. "Now."

"I'm not ready to scream yet." She stared down at the man who knelt by her bed, his arms bound behind his head. "You're not exactly in a position to challenge me."

His blew a slow, steady stream of air against the place that craved his mouth, and she moaned.

"I can keep going," he said. "Teasing you, pushing you to the edge and then pulling back, or you can say my name as you come hard and fast. I can take you there, Lena."

"Cocky," she murmured.

"That's a lesson for another day." He smiled up at her, the position she'd chosen highlighting his biceps. Goodness, those biceps. She drew her lower lip into her mouth, wondering how they'd feel.

"What do you say, Lena? You want more?"

"Yes," she said. "Please, Chad. *Please.*"

He lowered his head and started stroking her clit in earnest. As if he was using her needy, pleading sounds as a road map, he learned what she liked, how to vary the pressure to drive her out of her mind. Her hips rocked against his mouth, his tongue, silently begging for more. And he delivered, taking her to a place that felt free from everything but the pleas and the sound of his name.

Chapter 12

Chad walked around the helicopter. At one time, this tandem rotor, heavy-lift Chinook had ferried soldiers and supplies in a war zone. But it had spent the past few years hauling limber. And the California logging company that had gone belly-up thanks to the sluggish economy had stripped the bird down to the metal frame.

He ran his hand over the exterior. “Perfect.”

“Glad you approve.” Eric stood a few feet away, arms folded across his chest. “I sent the final payment yesterday. Moore Timber now owns two working helicopters, plus that heap of junk you insisted on buying for parts, and we still have only one pilot on staff.”

“I ran into Luke Murphy at the gas station this morning. He's interested in picking up some shifts,” Chad said, struggling to keep his voice serious. After talking to Luke in the checkout line, he'd damn near skipped back to his pickup.

Not that Luke deserved all the credit. The memory of the beautiful woman on her knees with her lips around his cock played a large part in his good spirits this morning. And the way, Lena had screamed his name while he'd rocked her world; yeah that was icing on the cake that left him skipping like a giddy schoolgirl.

"Is he qualified?" Eric asked, drawing Chad's wayward mind away from Lena's orgasms.

"Luke flew in the air force, so I'm confident in his skills, and he grew up around here, so he knows the business."

"Does he have a sister?"

"It shouldn't matter now," Chad said. "I took myself off the market like you suggested. I'm seeing someone."

"Lena Clark. I heard. And I saw enough last night when you picked her up to know it's more than a rumor." Eric turned his attention back to the helicopter. "I guess you're right. It might work out with Luke."

"What? You're not going to lecture me on how I shouldn't screw around with Lena? How I shouldn't hurt her after what she's been through?"

Eric raised an eyebrow. "Are you messing with her?"

"No," he said evenly. They'd laid out the terms of their deals. He belonged to her at night and she pretended to be his during the day.

"But that didn't stop Katie from threatening me," Chad added.

"I'm willing to bet Lena is stronger than you think," Eric said. "If you screw up, I won't be the one to kick your ass. Neither will Katie or Georgia. Lena can do that all by herself."

Chad's phone vibrated against his thigh. Pulling it out of his pocket, he glanced at the screen. His home phone number. "Excuse me, Eric. This might be Brody or Katie calling about my brother."

"Chad?" Lena's voice erased the oh-shit-did-something-happen-to-Josh feeling.

"Hey Lena, how's my girl today?" He walked away from the helicopter.

"I have an interview." Excitement disrupted her calm, in-control voice.

"That's great," he said, his mind stuck on the fact that she'd called him to share the news. Or maybe she'd started with Georgia and Katie, crossing them off one by one until she reached "fake boyfriend" on her list of go-to contacts.

"It's today at four," she added.

"I'll go with you," he said at the same time she asked, "Would you come—"

She broke off, ending her incomplete question with a laugh. "Thank you. It's the first interview since I started looking. I'm a little nervous."

"You're taking Hero?"

"Yes. Maybe." She paused, drawing a deep breath. "It would probably be better if I left him in the truck."

"I'll stay with him. Keep Hero company while you're inside. And afterward we'll celebrate. I know just the place."

"You don't have to do that," she said. "And I'm not big on fancy restaurants."

"Good." He glanced over at Eric. "I'm not taking you to one. But trust me, beautiful, you'll like this surprise."

"I might not get the job," she said.

"We'll celebrate either way," Chad said, the plan taking shape in his mind. He dropped his voice lower, not wanting Eric to overhear. "Where I'm taking you, Lena, you can call the shots. But when we get home tonight, it's my turn."

"WE'D LIKE TO hire a veteran."

The middle-aged man with a mustache and rotund belly designed to fill out a Santa suit raised his hand, rubbing the back of his balding head. Lena could feel the unspoken *but* hanging in the air, filling the cramped office. The wire factory covered a half-acre parcel on the Independence Falls town line, but the manager's workspace occupied only a fraction of the land.

"I served two tours in Afghanistan, sir," Lena said, her tone level and even. She stared at the manager's shiny head. He had no clue what it took for her to sit here, without Hero by her side. Every breath was measured and precise, focused on getting her through this interview without succumbing to panic.

"I believe I would be a good fit for your security team," she added.

The man shook his head. "When I posted the job, inviting veterans to apply, well, I'll be honest, I expected a man."

She bit back the words, *After serving on the front lines I think I can handle protecting the gate to your parking lot with a stun gun.*

"I know it sounds like a simple job," he continued. "But we had someone try to break in and steal a spool of cooper wire. In a truck."

Lena blinked. Clearly a *man* who'd served in the military could have stopped the truck. But a woman could probably only handle a compact car. Because the U.S. armed forces only handed out the stop-a-truck-with-a-stun-gun superpowers if you had a penis.

"Copper is valuable," Mr. Shiny Head continued, refusing to look her in the eye. "And right now there are a lot of desperate people out there."

"I see." She rose from her chair, refusing to let this man see even a hint of her own anxious need—not to steal, but to find a job. And maybe rekindle her pride along the way. "Thank you for your time, sir."

Her heartbeat raced as she turned to the door. But this time, fear took a backseat to the anger rising up. She needed to get out of here before she said something she might regret. And she wanted Hero by her side. Leaving her dog in the parking lot with Chad no longer seemed like a good call now that she knew she'd never had a shot at impressing this man. Because when Mr. Shiny Head looked at her, he saw a woman first, and a veteran second.

Lena closed the door behind her, resisting the temptation to slam it, and marched down the hall, her gaze focused on the exit. There had been a time—back when she wore the uniform and did her job alongside the other men and women willing to sacrifice everything, including their lives, to serve their country—when the people she worked with saw only one thing when they looked at her. Soldier.

She'd wanted to return to civilian life. She'd dreamed about it. But some days, like today, she missed the sureness of knowing she belonged.

Lena stepped into the parking lot and spotted Chad sitting in his truck with Hero at his side, the windows rolled down. Both males spotted her at the same time. Hero stood, struggling to maneuver his large body in the front seat, his tail wagging fast and furious, practically shaking the truck.

"That was fast. How'd it go?" Chad asked as she climbed into the passenger seat. "Did you get the job?"

"No." She wrapped her arms around Hero, holding him close, no longer caring if dog hair covered the slacks and button-down shirt she'd worn for the interview. "When they said veteran, they meant a man."

Chad's smile vanished. His hands gripped the steering wheel, hard, his knuckles turning white. His jaw clenched and his gaze shifted to the door. For a man who claimed he didn't play the part of the alpha male hero, Chad Summers looked ready and willing to introduce Mr. Shiny Head to his fist.

Lena tensed, prepared to stop him from fighting her battles. That fell beyond the barriers of their temporary agreement. And even if this were real, she didn't need him to stand up for her.

"Tell me something, Lena," he said, his voice a low rumble. "Can you do this job? Are you qualified?"

"Yes."

"Would it scare you to be out here late at night?" he challenged. "Would you need Hero at your side?"

"I never had a chance to mention Hero." She ran her hand over the dog's soft coat. "But no, I'm not afraid."

Because sometimes need trumped fear. And she needed this job. She needed to feel as if she could take a meaningful step forward.

He nodded, leaning back, releasing his death grip on the wheel. "Then it's a good thing you haven't given up on yourself isn't it?"

Her hand moved to the door, determination rising. She'd *fought*, dammit. She'd run into the fire. She'd done her job. And she could do this one.

Lena opened the truck door and stepped down, waiting for Hero to follow. "I'm going back in there."

Chad smiled and she swore she saw pride in his easygoing, charm-your-pants-off expression. "Damn right you are."

Standing tall, she marched past the parked cars, Hero at her side. Maybe she couldn't change the manager's mind. Maybe he'd throw her and her dog out. But she refused to walk away feeling somehow less than the men she'd served with because she was a woman.

CHAD HAD A list a mile long of what made a woman sexy. But right now, watching Lena march into that jackass's office, determination topped the chart. It outshone the natural beauty that could have landed her on the pages of a magazine—at least in his opinion. And yeah, maybe he was reading the wrong kinds of magazines to make a solid judgment, but right now, it didn't matter. When Lena had every reason to quit, she'd gone back inside, determined to fight.

"That's my girl," he murmured to the empty car.

For a split second, he'd debated going in there and throwing a few punches. But this was Lena, the woman who'd pushed forward, fighting her way toward the life she wanted when others had written her off. If she could survive two tours in Afghanistan—which was a helluva lot more than his zero—she could take on some paper-pushing jerk. She didn't need him to fight her battles.

Chad stared at the door leading into the office building as that realization sank in. Lena didn't need him. That was a good thing, wasn't it? No strings, no promises, a cut-and-dried deal—

The door swung open and Lena marched out, Hero at her side. Long hair flowing behind her, her stride strong and sure, an I-just-kicked-some-ass expression on her face—most guys would run for the hills. But Chad just stared.

He waited until she opened the truck door and climbed inside behind Hero before he asked, "How'd it go?"

"I made it clear to him that I don't accept failure as an option," she said, buckling her belt. "And I may have mentioned the Silver Star."

"So he's star-struck now, huh?" Chad turned the key and put the truck in reverse.

"Maybe," she said with a small smile. "Either way, I got the job. It's only part-time for now. Four nights a week, starting on Friday."

"But it's a start." He steered the truck down the main road. "Ready to celebrate?"

"Depends on what you have planned."

"If you don't like it, we can leave at anytime," he said, handing her his cell phone. "Do me a favor and call Georgia. Tell her we're on our way. She'll need to meet us at the gate. We can't get in without a member."

Lena touched the screen and scrolled through the numbers. "We're going to a country club?"

"Independence Falls doesn't have a country club, Lena. We're going to the Willamette Valley Gun Club."

Her brow furrowed as she held the phone to her ear. "You want to show off the fact that can I shoot?"

"No." He glanced over at the beautiful blonde in his passenger seat sitting tall and proud. "This is not part of the charade. This is for you. Because you went in there and you got the job."

Chad focused on the road, his jaw tight. Lena's new boss had no idea. When he'd offered the position, the jackass behind the desk had opened doors for her, and allowed her to reclaim herself.

"You did it, Lena." Chad accelerated down the empty road. "And I'm so damn proud of you."

Chapter 13

"We would need to stay behind the ready line," Georgia said, pointing to the yellow strip of paint on the cement floor about four feet behind a large, thick red line. Lena had jumped at the chance to shoot first, quickly selecting a pair of "ears" and "eyes," the protective gear required at the gun range. "But we can go out there and watch her."

"I'm fine to wait here." Chad nodded to the bulletproof glass separating the range from the spectators' area.

Georgia raised an eyebrow. "If you've given Lena a reason to point her revolver at you, we need to talk, Chad Summers. I'm not a marksman, so I'm guessing I'm not as good a shot as Lena, but I excel at hand-to-hand combat."

He glanced at the petite, brown-haired woman standing beside him. Growing up in the same town, he'd known Georgia most of his life. And he'd never thought of her as threatening—until now. Was it sending them into a war zone, training them to fight alongside men that brought out the fierce warrior in these women, or had the strength been there all along? he wondered.

"Shooters to the line," the range safety officer called from the other side of the window.

Lena stepped up to the red line, her gaze focused on the target in the distance. He suspected she'd always been strong. Serving her country gave her a way to show the world that she was a fighter. And a survivor.

"I'm doing my best not to hurt her," he said. "I want to be her friend, Georgia."

"Good." Georgia folded her arms across her chest. "She came here to find a better future for herself. Something more than the mess she left behind in Portland."

"Grass is greener on the other side and all that?"

Georgia nodded. "I want to make sure she finds what she is looking for. I know what it is like to come home and feel at loose ends. But for her it's worse."

"Because of her ex and her family," he murmured. The people who had given up on her.

But did the unknown on the other side promise a better future? He wouldn't know. His mother had never sent him a postcard from her new home after she'd run out on her family in search of greener pastures. For all he knew it was brown and barren.

And he'd never been one to walk away. When the going got tough—losing his father, watching his family's business slide toward financial ruin—he stayed, rooted to the one place he'd always called home. He stayed because he'd been the one left behind by a person searching for that something better, and it hurt like hell.

"Make ready," the range officer called.

Lena loaded her revolver, her movements quick and efficient. Would she find what she was looking for here? Or would she move on again? If she left town, it would be easier to end the relationship designed to fool his friends, and even his family.

But looking at Lena, and remembering the triumph in her bright blue eyes when she'd marched out of that office building earlier, he didn't want easy.

"Ready on the right," the officer called, scanning the line. The man in charge of the range paused, his gaze lingering on Lena. She was new. Of course the range officer would pay her extra attention.

And she was flat-out gorgeous.

"Ready on the left," the officer called. Chad searched his memory, trying to recall if he'd met the guy before.

"What's his name?" he asked Georgia, nodding to the tall, blond man with the broad shoulders. And when the hell had he ever noticed another man's freaking shoulders before?

"Who?" Georgia asked.

"Commence firing!" the blond-haired officer called.

"Him," Chad said as a series of gunshots rang out. Through the window, he watched Lena hold her arms steady as she fired once, twice, three times at the target. After five shots, she lowered her weapon, removed the empty chamber, and set both pieces on the table. He caught the small smile on her face. But one glance at the range officer and Chad knew he wasn't the only one looking.

"Cease firing!" the man called. The gunshots came to an abrupt halt, and he added, "Clear the line!"

"The guy calling out the instructions out there," Chad added. "The one looking at Lena."

"Oh, that's Noah. He lives a few towns over. His family owns Big Buck's, the nightclub near the university. I've never been, but Katie can tell you all about it. She took Liam there. Wild place."

"He runs a bar and works here?" Chad asked, tracking Noah's movements as the shooters stepped away from the line, and Noah headed over to the newcomer—Lena.

"He volunteers here. The members take turns working as the range safety officer. He's a marine, I think."

"Home on leave?" Chad asked.

"No, he's out," Georgia said as Noah stopped beside Lena, pointing out at the targets. "But once a marine, always a marine."

His brow furrowed. "Did she do something wrong?"

"Lena? I have a feeling she hit the target five times and probably left one hole. He's probably complimenting her."

Lena smiled up at broad-shouldered Noah. And shit, the man stepped closer. Hero, who'd patiently been waiting at Chad's side, put his front paws up on the windowsill and barked. Hell, Chad felt like barking too.

"He needs to move back," Chad said. "He's too close to her."

Georgia cocked her head to one side. "Chad Summers, are you jealous?"

"She doesn't like people getting too close," he said. "You know that. It's one of her triggers."

"I'll let Hero out." Georgia moved to the door, the anxious golden retriever following her. "If she starts to panic, he'll be there for her."

"Georgia, wait up," he said. "What are the rules here? Can you approach her?"

"We can go to her until the range safety officer calls shooters back to the yellow ready line," she said. "Why? Are you planning to warn Noah to stay away from Lena?"

"No." He scanned the room, spotted the clipboard hung on the wall, and headed over. "I want you to take Lena a note."

And remind Lena that she was *his*.

Georgia laughed. "Still using the same moves you used in high school?"

"I only wish I knew half the moves I know now, back when I was a teenager." He picked up the pen tied to the wall by the sign-in sheet. Rifling through his wallet, he found an old gas station receipt. He turned it over and started writing.

LENA GLANCED AT her gun resting beside the empty chamber. She wanted to reload and fire again, but she needed to wait for instructions. Down the line, the other shooters were removing their protective gear, congratulating one another on their performance. She didn't need anyone to tell her she'd hit the target. When it came to shooting, she didn't miss. Her pride swelled, and she knew it wasn't only linked to the five bullets she'd unloaded in the target.

Earlier, she'd stared failure in the face, and she'd walked away the winner. She'd ridden that high straight to the gun range. She felt at home here. She understood the rules. Holding her revolver, her gaze focused on the target, in that moment the anxiety receded. Maybe it was a lucky guess on Chad's part, but he'd picked the perfect place to celebrate.

"Hey there, new girl."

Her body shifted from calm and collected to alert in an instant. Looking away from her weapon, she spotted the tall, muscular man who'd called out the commands on the range. The words "Semper Fi" ran down his arm tattooed in red ink. A marine. Telling herself to relax, she smiled up at the man.

"Hi, I'm here with Georgia Trulane." She clasped her hands in front of her where he could see them. "If there's a problem—"

"No problem, sweetheart," he said with a smile that looked as if he'd been studying Chad's signature panty-melting grin. "Just wanted to welcome you to the Willamette Valley Gun Club. Either you're a natural or someone taught you how to take out a target."

"My dad," she said. "And after that West Point."

"Oh yeah? Seeing the way you shoot, I think I made a mistake joining the marines. I'm Noah."

"Lena." She nodded to her gun. "I'd like to shoot another round—"

"Great job!" A beaming Georgia moved to the marine's side, resting her hand on his arm as Hero pushed past them. The golden retriever stood by her side, his body pressed against her legs as if he wanted to reassure her that he was here for her. But Hero's gaze was fixed on Noah.

"I'll have to bring you back here again," Georgia continued. "But right now, I think we need to head out. Your boys are getting restless."

"My boys?" Lena searched her friend's face, looking for a clue.

Georgia nodded to the viewing area where Chad stood with his arms folded across his chest, no sign of his charm-your-pants-off smile. Maybe Noah hadn't learned the look from Chad. Maybe he'd stolen it.

Hero dropped the well-chewed duck and licked her hand, reminding her of her other "boy."

"He wanted me to give this to you." Georgia held out a folded scrap of paper with the local gas station logo on the front.

Lena unfolded the receipt and read the neatly printed words on the back.

Take what you need from me, beautiful. Give the orders and I'll follow you wherever you want to go. But remember when you come, I want to hear you scream my name.

Heat rose in her cheeks as she quickly folded the paper, hiding his words. She glanced at the window. Chad hadn't moved an inch, but he wasn't staring at her now. He was looking at Noah as if he wanted to have a conversation that started with threats and ended with *She's mine.*

But she wasn't his. It was only an illusion. Chad understood the boundaries, didn't he? Possession wasn't part of their pretend relationship.

Or maybe he was worried she'd jeopardize the charade.

"I'll get my gun," she murmured, picking up the revolver and the box of bullets Georgia had given her when they arrived. After everything Chad had done for her in the past few days, she refused to throw a wrench into their plan. "You're right, I think the shooting is making Hero nervous."

"Next time leave your boys at home," Noah said. "Be my guest and we'll shoot a few rounds. Army versus marines. We'll see who comes out on top."

"Thanks, but I don't go anywhere without Hero," she said.

"Noah, if you need someone to prove the army's better," Georgia jumped in. "I'm in."

Noah laughed, shaking his head as he headed back to his position between the left and right sides of the range. "Georgia, I've seen the way Eric looks at you. It's not much different than the pissed-off 'boy' behind the glass over there. And while Chad Summers isn't the possessive type, I can't say the same for your fiancé."

"Eric knows I can look out for myself," Georgia said, her hands on her hips.

Turning to the small structure that housed the viewing area, Lena left them to their argument. She opened the door, the words "not the possessive type" fresh in her mind. One look at Chad's stern expression and she wondered if this town had sorely misjudged him.

"I'm ready to head out," she told Chad.

"This is your night, Lena," he said, his attention focused on her, not the range safety officer. "You can stay for another round."

She shook her head. Through the open doorway, she could hear Georgia giving the marine shit. She walked up to Chad and placed her hand on his chest. "I'm not going to give anyone a reason to question what's between us. We've started enough rumors, Chad. I know you want to get up in the air, flying your helicopter over the forest. And I understand dreams. I know what it feels like to want something that is held just beyond your reach. So until you are back in that helicopter, living and breathing your dream, I'm yours."

She stepped closer, dropping her voice just in case Georgia chose that moment to come back inside. "You don't need to play the part of the jealous boyfriend. I'm going home with you."

"I'm not the jealous type." He raised his hand, covering hers.

"Are you sure about that?" She stepped closer, invading his space in a way that sent her pulse racing. Hero pressed against her legs and whined. But she refused to back down. She knew what she wanted. And she'd come too far to fail now. Normal was within reach. She could feel it, brushing her outstretched fingertips. One step forward and she could grab ahold of it.

"I saw the way you looked at the pretty pink toy you bought me," she added.

His sour attitude vanished, replaced by wanting. "I'm not going to lie. I want to be the one inside you. But I stand by what I said before, you call the shots, Lena. I'll follow your lead, wherever that takes us."

"Chad?" She leaned closer and whispered, "No more toys."

She shifted back, watching his face as that flash of kiss-me-now tenderness slipped away, replaced by his laughter.

"Beautiful, I've never been so damn happy to hear those words."

Chapter 14

LENA CLIMBED INTO the truck first, sliding across the bench and claiming the middle seat. "Hero can have the window."

Chad held the driver's door open, one foot on the gate, prepared to climb up. "You're sure about this?"

She nodded. "I'll roll the window down for him. I think he'll like having the wind in his face."

"Yeah, not what I meant." Chad settled into the driver's seat, securing his belt as he turned the key. They were on the main road, stopped at a red light, when she placed her hand on his thigh, and felt the muscles beneath his jeans tense.

"Lena," he said, his voice filled with warning as the signal turned green and he pressed on the gas.

"You're speeding."

"I'm not going to lie." He accelerated through a yellow light. "I'm a little anxious."

"Me too."

He turned down the driveway, raced past the farmhouse, and parked at an angle that would probably leave his siblings wondering if he'd come home drunk or too desperate to care. She knew he was stone-cold sober, so that left her with desperate—for her.

"We don't have to do this, Lena." He kept his gaze straight ahead. "You have nothing to prove to me."

"No, I don't. But I have a lot to prove to myself," she said. "I stayed locked in my home, away from everyone, for a long time. I was scared anything and everything would lead to a panic attack. But now, most of the time, I'm fine."

She drew a deep breath, knowing there was more she needed to say. "I might fall apart tonight. The panic might win. This is new ground for me. At least since I've been back. And if that scares you, or turns you off, Chad, you need to tell me."

"Move your hand, Lena," he said. "Up my leg."

She obeyed, drawing her fingers up his jean-clad thigh until they brushed the hard length pressing against his jeans.

He turned, his brown eyes staring into hers. "Lena, I'm dying to follow you up those stairs and into your bed. Whatever happens after that . . . it doesn't frighten me. It just means tonight is not our night. It won't keep me from looking forward to tomorrow, or the day after that, or the week after that. I'm not going to let you down, Lena. And I'm not going to run away."

His mouth formed a straight line, not a hint of a smile, as he waited for her to say something. This wasn't Chad the Charmer, using his words to send her tumbling head-first into lust-now-think-later territory. He meant what he said. The way he looked at her—it was as if he believed in her. And he wouldn't stop if she felt apart tonight.

Of all the people in her life, how had this man become the one who believed she could crawl her way back from every attack, every setback? How had Chad Summers found the words she'd wanted to hear for so long?

"Lena? You still with me?" His tone bordered on light and teasing. "Or should I start daydreaming about tomorrow night?"

"You mean that, don't you? You'll wait if I step out of this truck, freak out, and end up on my back in the dirt with Hero lying on top me?"

He took her hand, slowly and gently moving it away from his erection. Interlacing his fingers with hers, he smiled at her, soft and sweet. "Lena, do you know what I see when I look at you? I see a warrior. Even if you're lying on the ground beneath your dog, you're still a fighter."

"A warrior?" she repeated, turning the word over in her mind. She was proud of her strength and perseverance. But a warrior? "That doesn't sound sexy."

"You're a beautiful woman, Lena. But you're so much more than that." He reached out and tugged on a stray strand of hair that had fallen in her face. "I want to be the one who takes you to bed. It's not only about our deal, Lena. Not anymore. I meant what I wrote on that note. I want my name on your lips when you come. Again and again. And yeah, that is something I'm willing to wait for."

"Once you have me there, in bed," she murmured, a

rush of desire thrusting all other thoughts aside, "what do you plan to do with me?"

"Surprise." His signature smile returned. "Lead the way upstairs and you'll find out."

Raising an eyebrow, she reached across Hero and opened the door. Her dog jumped down first and she followed, leaving her bag with her revolver in the truck. She headed straight for the apartment before her courage failed her. But even if she lost it, her serene calm derailed by the feel of his body against her, hovering over her . . .

She froze, the key in the knob. Not over her. She didn't want him on top. Tonight, she wanted to the call the shots. She wanted to reclaim this part of her life. She wanted to claim *him*.

Unlocking the door, she led the way up to the bedroom, turning on the overhead light as she entered. She grabbed a reluctant Hero by the collar and led him to the bathroom, closing the door behind him.

"Did you mean the other stuff you wrote?" she asked, turning to face Chad. Standing inside the small studio, the bed to her back, she slipped off her shirt and tossed it aside. "On the receipt?"

"Yes." His hands went to the buttons on his flannel. "Take what you need from me."

Chad tossed the shirt aside, his hands moving to his belt, the same one she'd bound behind his head last night. Pants undone and low around his hips, he bent down to unlace his boots. He kicked them off, stripping away his remaining clothes.

Those chiseled abs, his hard, oh-so-impressive length—she might have a panic attack right now. And it would have nothing to do with post-traumatic stress. She wanted to touch, taste, and explore every inch of his body.

"I'm feeling very needy," she murmured, kicking off her shoes. The rest of her clothes followed. "Right now, I need you to lie down."

He walked around the other side of the bed, his brown eyes bright with mischief. Stretching out on his back, he placed his arms overhead.

"I'm ready, Lena." He didn't take his eyes off her as she knelt on the edge beside him. "Show me who you are. Before the war. After. Now. I want you."

Raising her hand, she trailed her fingers over his chest, outlining his perfect abs. Who was she? A woman who'd kept her desires and wants locked away, afraid that any little sound or movement would set off the internal alarm she'd carried home from Afghanistan.

But not tonight.

Her hand moved lower, wrapping around his cock, and her gaze followed. His hips lifted to meet her touch, a silent request for more, as Chad let out a shaky exhale. She looked up at his face, continuing to stroke him. The charismatic smile had slipped away, replaced by a rough, almost feral expression. He looked as if he was barely holding on to his control.

"Do you know what I want?" she said softly. "I want to feel you pressed against me." Her free hand moved between her legs, stroking her slick, sensitive clit. "Here."

Chad let out a low groan.

"Drives you wild, doesn't it," she said. "Having the tables turned?"

"Beautiful, you can talk dirty to me anytime." His body remained tense, his hips glued to the mattress. "But two can play at that game. My hands stay where they are."

"Good," she murmured.

"For now," he added. "But just say the word and I'll take over. I'd start by spreading your thighs."

She slid her knees across the bedspread, opening up to him as his words teased and toyed with her senses.

"That's it," he murmured, his focus on her fingers as her hips rocked into her touch. "Get close. But then I want you to stop. When you come, I want to be inside you, Lena."

"Yes." It was part cry, part whimper.

"Get there," he said, the rough edge to his voice highlighting his struggle to hold back. "To that point where you *need* me."

Need—the way he'd said that one word, as if it came from a place so elemental, so basic, it couldn't be denied.

"Now," she said. "I want you now."

If he said another word, she'd tumble into an orgasm. She took her hand off his cock, looking around the small space like a wide-eyed teenager who knew the next step, but was too overrun with wanting to think straight.

"There's a box of condoms in the nightstand," he said, his teeth clenched tight.

She found the box, quickly removing a strip, tearing one off. Returning to her perch on the bed, her legs trembling, not with fear, but desire to leap into the next moment. She covered him and settled one leg on either side of his hips. Holding him with one hand, she guided him inside, feeling every inch.

"Wow," she murmured, leaning her head back.

"Don't close your eyes," he said. "Please. I need to know you're right here with me."

Lifting her head, she met his intense gaze. She began to move, riding him at her pace, taking her time, savoring the slow build to the end.

Anxiety waited on the perimeter, making way for a rainbow of emotions. Desire chased by reckless, wanton abandon as her hips rocked faster and harder, craving the physical rush of sensations.

"Chad," she cried. "Oh God, Chad."

In that moment, as she floated off into orgasmic bliss, staring into his wide-eyed, wild gaze, touching him, feeling him beneath her . . . in that moment, she felt at home with her feelings. That sensation might be as fleeting as her orgasm, but she'd take it. For now, this was enough.

HEARING HER SCREAM his name, watching her let go of the control that boxed her in and also kept her holding on, he wanted more. He held back, unwilling to barrel toward the finish line now that she'd come.

Slowly, the sexy chant of "Chad, oh God, Chad" faded and her movements slowed. She smiled down at him, her long hair falling forward, obscuring his view of her breasts as she pressed her palms against his chest. Keeping his hands on the headboard, he fought the urge to move his arms and brush it away.

"Your turn," she murmured, her fingertips tracing light, teasing circles around his nipples. "Are you ready?"

He thrust his hips up into her, reminding her of his hard, aching cock buried deep inside her. "What do you think?"

"I think I want to hear you scream my name now." Sitting up, she started to move, running her hand up to her breasts, covering them, teasing them. Every moment brought him closer.

"Stop holding back," she ordered.

"Lena," he growled, wanting more—everything she had to give. "You're so damn beautiful."

She drove him wild, offering everything she could, pushing the boundaries without breaking apart. He took it. Letting go. He lost himself in her beauty, in the roaring, demanding lust, in her—and something more—something that tugged at his heart. His last thought as he came, calling her name . . . what would happen when she left?

He closed his eyes, pushing the questions away. Right now, he had her and he'd take whatever she was willing to give.

"Chad?" she murmured. "Still with me?"

"Yeah." He opened his eyes, struggled to get his ragged breathing under control. "I'm with you."

Slowly, she broke their intimate contact, moving to the edge of the bed. "Do you need me to go get Hero to help calm you down?"

He reached over, grabbed a pillow, and tossed it at her. "I don't need your dog, Lena." Slowly, he lowered his arms, allowing the blood to return to his hands. He patted the bedside next to him. "I want you."

He watched her chest rise as she sucked in a deep breath and held it, her fingers curling into the pillow he'd tossed at her.

"But maybe you should go check on your four-legged friend?" he said, offering an out. One look at her white knuckles and he knew cuddling pushed the limits.

The familiar sound of his cell phone filled the studio apartment. Chad sat up, swinging his legs over the edge of the bed.

"I'd ignore it," he said, retrieving the phone from the pile of discarded clothes. "But—"

"Your brother is still in the hospital," she said, freeing Hero. "I understand."

He nodded, touching the screen before raising the phone to his ear. "Chad here."

"Hey, it's Eric. Glad I caught you."

"What's up?" He moved to the kitchenette, his brow furrowed with concern. "Did Georgia make it home all right? When we left the range, she was still there."

"She's in the kitchen making dinner right now," Eric said. "I'm calling with some good news. Luke took the job and he can start tomorrow."

"So we're green-lighted to fly?"

"Yes," Eric said. "I know it's short notice, but I could use you on the harvest site north of town. I thought you could take your new copilot for a test flight tomorrow and then head over there and check out the site, talk to the crew chief."

"Yeah, I can do that," he said, trying not to sound like a kid who'd been offered the freaking keys to the candy store. This was it. His dream, his dad's dream, transforming into reality. "Tell Luke I'll meet him at the helicopter bright and early."

Chad ended the call and turned to face Lena. She'd slipped her dress on while he'd been on the phone, and Hero sat by her side.

"I guess this means the plan worked," she said, her left hand reaching for her golden retriever.

Her words thrust his dream aside, his present, Lena, shifting to the forefront. He wasn't ready to let her go. "Yeah. It worked," he said. "How about we celebrate over pizza?"

She smiled and her hand fell away from the dog. Yeah, he had a hunch she wasn't ready to walk away from their deal yet either.

"We wouldn't want everyone to think you'd fallen into your old habits as soon as you found a copilot," she said.

"Not when we've come this far."

Lena nodded, glancing at the window.

"We can grab a pie to go," he said, knowing it would be too dark by the time they reached A Slice of Independence to sit outside. And a crowded restaurant might be too much for one day. "Cheese, pepperoni, or the special."

"Put on your pants, Chad." She nodded to his clothes. "And then we'll negotiate."

He obeyed, pulling on his clothes. "I like it better when you tell me to take them off."

"Me too," she said. "Me too."

Chad followed her out the door and down to his pickup. She was still his. But someday their little game would end.

Chapter 15

"How long do you think we can keep this up?" Chad asked, his stride slow and lazy despite her rushed steps down Independence Falls's Main Street.

After seven days helicopter logging at a remote job site, her pretend boyfriend had returned home ready to kick back and relax. Lena had the day off, her work schedule still limited to the Friday through Monday overnight security shifts, but she also had plans.

"As long as we need to." Lena glanced at her watch. Georgia and Katie would be at the nail salon right now. They could get started without her. Lena had no intention of parting with her hard-earned dollars for a coat of polish delivered by a nosy stranger. But she'd promised she'd meet them there to talk about Georgia's wedding plans.

"It's been three weeks," Chad said. "You're not tired of me yet?"

"I haven't seen you in seven nights."

"You're right. I think it might take a while longer." He stopped in front of Ariel's Salon, wrapping his arm around her waist and drawing her close. He touched his lips to hers, stealing a quick kiss.

But she wanted more, so much more. She ran her fingers through his hair, capturing his mouth, her tongue touching his as she deepened the kiss.

"Lena," he said, breaking away. "We're on Main Street."

"Hmm." She brushed his lips over his again. "Georgia and Katie might be peeking through the salon window. I wouldn't want them to think you found someone else while you were away."

"There's no one else, Lena."

"I'm glad I'm your only fake girlfriend," she teased, resting her forehead against his.

"Lena—"

"I should go in," she said, breaking free from his hold. At some point they needed to talk about how to end the charade, but not yet. "They're waiting for me."

"Are you ready for our road trip Thursday?" he asked.

She nodded. He'd scheduled three days off to drive her down to the medal ceremony. She'd done the same, knowing she'd lose two nights' pay to make the trip. But the medal had helped her land the job. And her family would be there. Plus the vice president and the media . . . Hero pressed close as if sensing her rising panic.

"We're meeting my parents and my brother for dinner Thursday night," she said, focusing on the concrete details. "So we'll need to leave early. They picked a Chinese restaurant not far from the motel. The Red Dragon."

"Sounds great, Lena."

She blinked. It sounded like hell to her. But Chad hadn't met her family yet.

"I look forward to meeting them," he added.

"My dad," she said, knowing she needed to give him a warning. "He's not easy. Most people don't like him. And—"

"Don't worry about me. I have charm on my side, remember?"

She frowned. Maybe this was a horrible idea. "It won't work on him."

"Go meet Georgia and Katie." He nodded to the salon. "Talk wedding plans. I'll swing by and pick you up for dinner later. Around six?"

Lena nodded, her hand brushing Hero's coat.

"And Lena, stop worrying about Thursday."

He turned and headed down street, waving to Trish as she set the picnic tables for the lunch rush.

Chad walked as if the road in front of him was paved with rainbows and sprinkled with fairy dust. He lived in a fairy-tale world, one she'd caught a glimpse of but could no longer enter. The land of once-upon-a-time was in her past, divided from the rocky, uncertain path in front of her.

Lena glanced down at the dog leaning against her legs as if trying to hold her up. Kneeling, she wrapped her arms around Hero. "I'm OK," she murmured. "Just daydreaming about following Chad Summers to the pot of gold at the end of the rainbow. I know he'll find his way. He's got charm on his side."

Hero licked her face.

"And I've got you," she added, tightening her hold on the dog. "We'll get where we're going. But I have a feeling success for us looks a little different than it does for him."

She stood and headed inside the salon. Later, she could worry about the medal ceremony. Right now, she needed to focus on white dresses and wedding cake. If she let her friendship with these two women slide, her future in Independence Falls would look bleak and lonely when Chad Summers reached the end of the road with her and went on his merry way.

TWENTY MINUTES LATER, Lena sat in an overstuffed chair, sipping green tea. The recent dose of fall weather ruled out sitting on the salon's back patio while Georgia and Katie waited for their nails to dry. Instead, they'd claimed a quiet corner inside Ariel's Salon.

"I'm moving up the wedding," Georgia announced. "Eric plans to log all winter now that the helicopter operation is up and running. He says he makes more per log this time of year, so I said go for it. We'll get married in December, time the wedding with the year-end accounting when everything slows down."

Katie nodded, admiring her shiny red nails. "It does. But December is weeks away. You need to find a dress and a venue. Unless you're thinking Vegas?"

"No." Georgia shook her head. "I think we're going to have a small ceremony and reception in the backyard by the pond."

"You still need a dress," Katie pointed out.

"I was hoping to do some shopping when I'm in Portland on Saturday." Georgia looked at her. "I thought I could use a little pick-me-up after our group therapy session."

Running a finger over her nails to check if the polish had dried, Katie nodded. "I'm in. For the shopping, not the therapy."

"I can't make it to the group meeting this week," Lena said. "We're driving back from the medal ceremony on Saturday."

"We?" Georgia wiggled her red toes. "Is your family bringing you back?"

Lena shook her head. She'd told her friends about the Silver Star—Georgia had jumped up and down with excitement, threatening to throw a party to celebrate—but Lena had left out some of the details.

"Chad is going with me," she said.

Katie stopped blowing on her fingernails and stared at Lena as if she'd announced her plan to run down Main Street naked. "You're taking my brother to meet your parents?"

"He volunteered to go to the ceremony," she said. "And I can't exactly leave him in the motel room while I eat with my family." Although that plan had merits. Then she wouldn't need to explain.

But he'd see her father and brother the next day, and then he'd know.

"That a big step," Georgia said, her brown eyes sparkling with delight.

"Do you think your father will hate him?" Katie demanded.

"Yes," Lena said.

Katie pointed one perfectly manicured nail at her. "Promise me that if you run off to city hall, you'll call first. I want to be there when my brother gets married. And you'll need witnesses. Lots of them if Chad's tying the knot."

Lena choked on a mouthful of hot tea. Coughing, she struggled to find her voice. "We're not getting married. We're not even—"

Dating.

She couldn't say the word, revealing their plan to Georgia and his sister. Chad's dream had turned into reality. He was flying. Even when they staged a breakup and went their separate ways, she couldn't reveal the truth and put everything he'd hoped for at risk.

"I'm not interested in marrying anyone right now," she said.

"Lena, I know, believe me I do, that you have a lot to deal with right now," Georgia said. "But life is too short to second-guess happiness."

"I know." Lena stared out the window at the mountain peaks. "And I'm getting there, bit by bit. But it's a long battle."

And it was one she refused to lose. But with Chad it was not a question of winning or losing—because she couldn't claim a victory when the prize was merely an illusion.

"Right now, I just need to get through the next few

days." Lena turned to Georgia. "And you need to buy a wedding gown. Do you have any ideas or should we start tearing out pages from bridal magazines?"

On Thursday evening, Lena followed the waiter to the far corner of the Red Dragon's elaborately decorated dining room. Her steps were slow, as if she were trudging through ankle-deep sand, wishing she could fast-forward hours into the future.

"We could skip dinner and go straight to the bedroom at the motel," she whispered.

Chad took her hand, probably to ensure she didn't run for the door before they saw the menu. "We've been driving for eight hours. I need egg rolls before sex." Raising his voice, he called to the waiter: "How are the egg rolls?"

Ignoring the answer, Lena studied the space. Red walls lined with gold trim suggested this was a step up from the Asian take-out in Independence Falls. But unlike the fancy Chinese food place near her old home in Portland, the large dining room was mostly empty.

"We're ten minutes early," she said when they reached the circular table in the far corner of the restaurant.

"We'll order some starters." Chad walked around, selecting two seats that faced out, the backs against the wall. "Your folks had a long trip from Texas, I bet they'll be hungry too."

Sitting down, she ran her hands over her long skirt, smoothing the fabric. Wearing his service dog vest, Hero remained glued to her side, hidden from view by the large table.

"Before my family arrives," she said, "I should warn you—"

"You dad will hate me from the moment he walks in?" Chad accepted a menu from the waiter. "Your brother will demand to know my intentions? Don't worry, Lena. I'd do the same in his shoes. Ask Liam. When he started seeing Katie again, I tried to start the conversation with my fists. But I'm guessing your family might be a little more civilized. Especially if there is food on the table when they arrive."

Lena shook her head. "My brother stopped trying to defend my honor years ago. Joe doesn't think like that."

Her brother treated her like a soldier, and he expected her to behave like one. The same went for her father. They refused to accept any signs of weakness. They had fought, suffered, and pushed through it. And they were baffled when she'd failed to do the same.

"Joe and I were never close growing up," she added. "And when he left the military and moved back home, I was already deployed."

"Joe lives in Texas too?" Chad asked, scanning the menu.

"Down the street from my parents in the town where we grew up." She drew a deep breath as a tremor ran through her body. Hero rested his head in her lap.

"Lena," Chad said. "Don't worry about it. Even if they hate me, we'll survive dinner. I promise."

"But I should have warned you in the car," she said quickly, hating the trembling in her voice. "I should have—"

"I don't need warnings, Lena."

"But—"

"Right now, Hero is thinking about climbing onto your lap and making you do some deep breathing exercises." Chad nodded to her dog without taking his eyes off the menu. "I think we need to focus on two things, breathing and food."

"You can read my dog's mind now?"

Hero lifted his head and looked at Chad. She could have sworn the golden retriever smiled at him. Over the past few weeks, her pseudo-boyfriend and her service dog had grown close, becoming a team. The Keep Lena From Freaking Out Duo. It was sweet, but also disheartening to admit she needed so much help. Still. After being home for a year and a half. A point her father would likely drive home over egg rolls.

Chad reached under the table and took her hand in his. "I can read you, beautiful. And I think you might want a drink to go along with the appetizers."

Pressing her lips together, she shook her head. "I can't drink tonight."

"I'm driving." He raised his free hand and waved to a waiter. "Have whatever you want."

Lena listened, her gaze focused on the front door as he ordered enough food for an army and a glass of wine for her. His thumb traced soft circles on the palm of her hand while he spoke. And Hero nudged her with his nose, demanding attention. Sandwiched between Hero and Chad, her nervous energy gradually subsided.

She could do this. Whether she liked the fact that she needed them or not, her team was here. And this was just dinner in a quiet, nearly empty restaurant. She could—

The front door opened. A tall, slim woman with gray hair that Lena knew had been the same blond as hers once upon a time maneuvered a wheelchair through the door. In the chair sat the tall, proud man whose words still haunted her. His darker coloring presented a sharp contrast to his wife.

"My dad injured his spine during a training accident," she said softly, knowing the explanation came too late. "It happened when I was twelve."

Her gaze shifted to the tall, smiling man behind her parents. Her brother wore long pants, but when he moved, she caught a glimpse of his prosthetic.

"And my brother lost his leg in Iraq. IED. His convoy was hit," she explained quickly as the waiter guided her family to their quiet corner of the Red Dragon.

Chad nodded, his mouth forming a thin line as he pushed back from the table and stood to greet her family.

"And after Joe came home, you went over there to fight," he said, his voice soft. But there was a hard edge in his tone. "You went knowing your brother had lost his leg."

"Yes." She rose to greet the family she hadn't seen in months. "And I'm the one who fell apart."

"You're putting yourself back together too," he murmured. "Don't forget that."

She glanced up at Chad, expecting to find him studying her family. But he wasn't. Chad was looking at her.

"Remember, Lena," he said softly. "You set the boundaries and the limits. If this is too much, we'll take the egg rolls and run."

Chapter 16

"RUNNING OFF WITH the food?" Her lips offered the faintest hint of a smile. "Not exactly the way to win over my father."

"I'm not here for your father's approval. I'm here for you."

The weight of those words sank in. Chad was surrounded by real-life heroes—shit, he was the only man at their table who could walk on his own two feet—and determined to be hers. He wanted to see Lena through tonight. And he'd do whatever it took to bring her home with the medal she deserved.

Looking around the table, he'd never felt less qualified for the part. He'd never put his life on the line for his country. But he'd stuck by his family. He'd been there for his brothers and sisters. Hell, half the time Katie hadn't wanted him butting his nose into her business, but that hadn't stopped him from trying to look out for her.

He'd stand by Lena tonight. He might not be her hero, or even her boyfriend, but their friendship? That was real.

Lena made the introductions, not once touching or hugging her parents or brother. Watching the scene unfold, Chad had a bad feeling charm would not be on his side tonight.

"We're happy to meet Lena's new friends." Lena's mother, Alice, spoke with a thick Texas accent, a soft smile on her lips as she glanced at her daughter.

"Chad." Mr. Rodriguez said his name as if it was somehow lacking. "How did you meet Lena?"

Chad smiled, biting back the words, *My family stepped in to help your daughter after you gave up on her.* Picking a fight before the egg rolls arrived wouldn't help Lena. She was already a ball of trembling nerves. One glance at her lap and he saw Hero now had his head and one paw resting against her leg.

"I was worried when she moved away from her life in Portland," Mrs. Rodriguez added.

Maybe they'd tried. But it wasn't enough. When it came to family, you didn't give up and you didn't walk away. Family was the glue that held life together when everything else fell apart, not the ones standing on the sidelines playing the part of spectators.

"Lena moved into the apartment over our barn," he said. "Once I saw how good she is with a gun, well, I decided I wanted to get to know her better. So I asked her out, and lucky for me, she said yes."

"You're dating?" Lena's mother said, her smile widening.

"I'm a sucker for a beautiful woman," he said. "And now I see beauty runs in the family."

Charm might not work on her father, but Lena's mother flushed at the compliment.

The waiter interrupted, depositing two trays of mixed appetizers. Another followed with Lena's wine. Chad saw her father's brow furrow when the glass was placed in front of his little girl.

"I went ahead and ordered a few things to start," Chad said. "One plate is vegetarian."

"We love our meat down in Texas. But thanks, man, I can't wait to dig in. It was a long trip to get here. Three flights," Joe said, his voice light and friendly. But Chad could feel Lena's brother studying him closely.

"Lena," Mr. Rodriguez said as his wife filled his plate. "Have you given more thought to going back to the army? With a Silver Star—"

"No, Daddy, I'm not going back." Lena reached for her wine. "I found a position in Independence Falls."

"Doing what?" her father demanded.

Lena explained the details of her job as if she were reading the listing from the classified ads. She left out the battle she'd fought and won to secure the position.

"Security?" Mr. Rodriguez tossed the second half of his egg roll onto his plate as if the mention of her job stole away his appetite. "Lena, you went to West Point."

"I know." Lena raised her wine to her lips and took a long drink. "I pointed that out during the interview."

Mr. Rodriguez shook his head. "You were an officer in the United States Army."

"Yes, I was," she said. And this time, her voice trembled.

Chad stared across the table at the man who dared to dismiss Lena's accomplishments. How could anyone look at the woman sitting beside him and see failure? He reached for her, knowing she need support, not a friend who challenged her father. But Hero beat him to the punch, choosing that moment to climb into Lena's lap as if he were a Chihuahua. The golden retriever rested one paw on her shoulder and his head on the other side, as Chad held tight to the table's edge to keep it from tipping.

"Is that your new dog?" her mother asked.

Lena wrapped her arms around the retriever, clinging to him. "Yes."

Her father opened his mouth as if ready to offer his two cents on the subject when the waiter appeared.

"We're ready to order the main course," Chad said quickly. "Joe, are you still hungry?"

"You bet," Lena's brother said.

They went around the table placing orders. With her family's attention diverted to the mundane, Chad felt Lena relax. Hero abandoned his post at her shoulder. The big dog settled on her lap, determined to play the part of an animal a quarter his size to keep Lena calm. From what he'd witnessed of Lena's family so far, Hero's training would be put to the test tonight. No wonder she'd spent the past couple of days tied in knots over seeing her father. Warm and welcoming wasn't in the man's vocabulary.

Chad watched Lena as she spoke to the waiter. Maybe she had come to Independence Falls looking for greener grass. After seeing where she'd come from, hell, he couldn't hold that against her.

LENA HAD FACED armed insurgents determined to harm or capture her and her fellow soldiers. In Afghanistan, she'd fought to save the lives of the men and women fighting at her side, and defend her own. But sitting here, trembling with a dog in her lap, it was as if her bravery, her fearless ability to fight, her resilience, all existed in another world.

She glanced over at her father, his gaze fixed on the menu. He was so close. She could reach out and touch him. But first she'd have to break through the wall between them.

It felt as if her father had arrived at the Red Dragon with her brother, her mother, and his expectations. When he'd challenged her about her security job, she'd been tempted to ask if they should pull up a chair so his disappointment could have a place at the table.

But she knew better than to play the can't-you-see-I'm-suffering card with her father. Serving his country had left her dad confined to a wheelchair, and it had robbed his only son of a leg, yet she knew he'd do it all over again. For as long as she could remember, his willingness to sacrifice for their country had been a thing of awe and wonder. And she'd followed in his footsteps, ready and willing to serve.

Some days it was hard to admit that she had nothing left to give. To acknowledge to the brave men at this table that something as abstract as PTSD held her back when they had given physical parts of themselves to the fight. And it was just as difficult for her father to accept that fact.

"Did Joe tell you he competed in the Warrior Games?" her mom asked, the familiar sound of her Texas drawl reminiscent of the best parts of Lena's childhood.

Lena's eyes widened as she glanced at Joe. "No. You never mentioned a word."

Her big brother smiled. "I figured you had your hands full."

With her life falling apart?

"You should have called," she said. "Which sport?"

"He came in fourth in the shooting event." Her mom patted Joe's shoulder. "And he was second during the trials at West Point."

She remembered her mother mentioning a trip to West Point during one of their weekly calls back when she was living in Portland. But she'd been trying to adjust to having Hero in her life, and struggling to fix her crumbling marriage.

"It was fun," Joe said. "Good to be part of a team again. Next year, I'm going to enter the track and field events. I just got a new prosthetic designed for running. My times are even better than with my real leg."

"What doesn't kill you makes you stronger," Mr. Rodriguez announced to the table.

"I don't know about that, Daddy," she said softly, her smile vanishing. "I haven't felt strong in a long time."

Saying those words out loud, *to her father*, Lena felt as if the determination that she wore like body armor had been stripped away.

"I know, Lena, but you will be," her daddy said, his voice resolute as if she could erase her fears though sheer willpower. If only it worked that way. If she could wake up one day and push the fear, the hypervigilance, and the depression away, burying it in a game of mind over matter, she would.

"Tomorrow you're going to receive the army's third highest honor," her father continued. "And then maybe you'll consider going back. The army has resources for soldiers suffering from a little anxiety."

"Daddy, I didn't leave my house for three months. I pushed my husband away, my friends, everyone. I need a dog at my side to get through the day," she said, her voice rising with every word. "Tomorrow, I might run the other way when I see the stage and the crowd of people. I don't have a *little anxiety*. I'm buried in it. It's been suffocating me for months.

"Now that I'm finally on my way to a semi-normal life, a fresh start, no, I don't want to go back." Tears welled in her eyes. "I can't do it, Daddy. I'm sorry. I'm still alive, but I'm not strong. Not anymore."

The table fell silent, the three members of her family staring back at her. Her fingers brushed Chad's thigh as he raised his hand, signaling the waiter.

"Can we take ours to go?" Chad asked when the server appeared at his side.

"You're leaving?" her mom said, her tear-filled eyes wide with surprise.

"I just remembered a call I need to make," Chad said. "Business stuff."

"What line of work are you in?" her father demanded, his eyes narrowing on Chad before glancing at her. She debated running to the truck now that she'd delivered the speech that had been building inside her for the past year.

"Helicopter logging," Chad said with a smile, as if this was a logical reason for an abrupt departure. Under the table, he took her hand and squeezed.

"I'm just starting out really," Chad continued. "Before that my siblings and I ran the trucking company founded by my grandfather. We hauled timber mostly."

Chad kept talking, filling the void as they waited for their to-go bag. But Lena tuned him out, her father's words echoing in her head.

What doesn't kill you makes you stronger.

But what if tomorrow, on that stage, she turned into a puddle of weakness? What if it pushed her close to the point that she wished she'd given her life when she was at her strongest? What if even for the brief time it took to receive the award, she thought about giving up on herself?

Lena stared at the seventy-pound dog anchoring her to the chair when she wanted to run as fast as she could away from this restaurant, her family, and these feelings. If she gave up, there would be no one left holding on to the belief that one day she could reach out and touch normal again.

"Lena, are you ready?" Chad asked.

No one except him.

Chad pushed back from the table, a take-out bag in one hand. "I really do need to make that call."

"Yes." She nudged Hero and he hopped off her lap. Taking Chad's free hand, she stood, allowing him to lead her toward the door. But with each step the isolation mounted.

She couldn't count on the pretend boyfriend holding her hand. Their relationship was for show. She needed to rebuild her life on something solid. Glancing over her shoulder, she watched her family clustered together—three people at a table set for five. Maybe once upon a time, they had been her foundation. But now they wanted strength from her, not weakness. And she couldn't deliver.

Lena stepped out into the cool fall night. Darkness had descended on the sleepy little Oregon town near the army base. Chad beat her to the truck, opening the passenger side door for her.

"So what do you think," he said. "Did I make a good first impression?"

His teasing words were like a crutch, there to prop her up when her world started to crumble.

"You were memorable," she admitted, climbing up beside Hero. Chad walked around the front, settled into the driver's seat, and turned on the truck.

"I think your brother liked me," he said, steering onto the road.

"Joe is a friendly guy." She stared out the window as they turned onto the dark, country road. They'd driven past the motel on their way to the Red Dragon. Home for the night was a matter of retracing their steps for ten minutes. "He was like that before he deployed."

"Did he have a hard time after he lost his leg?"

"I don't know," she admitted. "He was in the hospital for a while, first in Germany and then at Walter Reed.

My mother flew over when they weren't sure if he would make it."

"Did she fly out to see you when you came back?"

She shook her head. "I wasn't injured. And I went to Texas a couple of weeks after my last tour ended. It's hard for them to travel. I had my first nightmare down there. My mom came into my room that night and held me."

Staring out into the night, she could still remember the feeling of her mother's arms around her, rocking her. She tried to push her away, but her mother had held on tight, softly signing the songs from her childhood.

"But you didn't stay," he said.

"I had a husband in Portland. I'd left the army expecting to start my civilian life, and then I just couldn't."

He nodded. "Do you want to wait here while I get our key?"

"Sure." She held tight to Hero as he slipped into the reception area. A few minutes later, Chad returned, smiling.

"Let me guess, you charmed your way into an upgrade," she said.

"Lena, this is the Roadside Motel. They don't do high-end," he said holding open her door. "But I confirmed that breakfast comes with the room."

He led the way down the open-air corridor to the last door. Inside, she surveyed the accommodations. When trying to find a place that took dogs, even service dogs, the options were limited, especially in her price range. Their assigned room was clean, with a king-size bed on the left, and a dresser to the right with a television perched on top. Beyond the dresser was an open door leading to the bathroom. She poked her head in. Small, but serviceable. She turned as Chad set their overnight bags down on the bed.

"How's the tub?" he asked. "Big enough for two?"

"It is, but . . ." She glanced at the hotel room, folding her arms across her chest. "I'm not sure we need to stay. I don't think I can get up on that stage. I ran out of dinner with my family, Chad. Hero sat on my lap through the meal and the place was practically empty. Tomorrow there will be people everywhere. Any little sound or movement could trigger a massive panic attack. And the thought of lying on the ground with my dog across my chest, trying to calm me down, while my family and a bunch of strangers watch . . ."

Chad faced her, hands at his side. "The medal is yours either way. You earned it. Don't think for a minute you've failed because you don't want to stand up there. And running out on your family tonight? You stopped me from doing something stupid, like telling a man in wheelchair to shut the hell up."

"He's not a bad person," she said. "My dad just had a plan for how our lives would be. But my dreams for the future are different now."

"Lena, can I ask you something?" He twirled the hotel room key around his finger. "Do you regret going to West Point, joining the army? Following your dad's dream?"

"Not for a minute," she said, her voice strong and clear. "I'm proud of the time I spent serving my country. Just not of what happened when I returned home. Maybe if this ceremony was a year from now. But tomorrow? I'm not ready. I need more time to put myself back together."

"OK. I've got to make a call." He smiled, but it didn't touch his brown eyes. She saw a laserlike focus in his gaze that looked foreign. But she knew, probably better than most people, that Chad was more than the party-hard, fun-loving guy.

"Stay here, take a shower, relax," he said. "And when I come back, I want you to take everything you need to make you feel strong. You know I'm game for anything. Handcuff me to the bedpost if you want."

"Handcuffs?" She raised an eyebrow, glancing at his bag.

"Whatever you want, beautiful."

CHAD HEADED FOR the main office, and the friendly redhead receptionist at the front desk.

"Hi Annie." He offered his best smile.

"Mr. Summers." The college-age woman looked up from the LSAT prep book open on the reception desk and beamed at him. "Is your room OK?"

"Just fine. But I was wondering if you could help me locate a phone number. We're in town for an event at the army base, but I forgot the paperwork at home. I'm not sure where to go in the morning and was hoping to call over there for some answers."

Annie frowned. "I don't have a number for the base, but my friend works over there. Are you in the army?"

"My girlfriend served," he said. "Can I give your friend a call?"

A minute later, he stepped outside, his cell pressed

against his ear, and began the long process of trying to get ahold of the person connected to the medal ceremony. Six transfers later, he reached the woman in charge.

"Hi, this is Chad Summers. I'm with Officer Clark." Shit, he couldn't even remember her rank. "We're in town for the Silver Star."

"Glad you made it," the sergeant on the other end of the line said, her tone formal and rushed.

"Here's the thing, Lena can't get up on that stage. I know you have press coming, but she suffers from PTSD, something I'm guessing you're familiar with. She's afraid she will panic when it is time to accept the medal."

"The vice president of the United States is flying in to present this medal—"

"Well, he's going to have to do it in a quiet room with only family a few others present. I don't care what it takes to rearrange the dog-and-pony show you have planned. Lena deserves to be honored in a way that makes her feel proud of her service."

"Are you family?" the woman demanded.

"No, I'm the guy who will move heaven and earth to make damn sure she is not afraid."

Chapter 17

LENA PACED BACK and forth across the motel's worn brown carpet. From his perch on the bed, Hero followed her movements. The golden retriever had walked at her side for the first five or so minutes after Chad left before deciding to save his energy. She should probably do the same, for tomorrow, or maybe later tonight . . .

I want you to take everything you need to make you feel strong. You know I'm game for anything. Handcuff me to the bedpost if you want.

She stopped and stared at the solid wood headboard, not a post in sight. But that wasn't the only thing holding her back. She couldn't continue to take and take from this man. Tonight had made it crystal clear that she needed to focus on her future. She couldn't afford failure. She just couldn't. She needed order in her life and people who didn't cling to fake girlfriends because commitment sent them racing for the door.

"Lena." She turned and saw the knob turn. Chad stepped inside, a devilish grin on his handsome face. "Beautiful, you don't look relaxed. Or ready for these."

He held out his right hand, a pair of toy handcuffs dangling from his index finger.

She raised an eyebrow. "Plastic handcuffs?"

"I bought them from toy store at the mall. I'm guessing they're left over from Halloween." He swung them back and forth like a pendulum. "Want to see if they'll hold?"

She laughed for the first time since they'd walked into the Red Dragon. They were barreling toward the end of their charade, but she couldn't walk away tonight. Not when he walked in and delivered laughter coupled with the promise of sex.

And handcuffs. She couldn't forget those.

"How about a game?" he said. "First one naked gets to try them on."

She raised an eyebrow, watching as he tossed the handcuffs on the bed and went to work removing his clothes. "The first one to wear them will be the only one."

Fingers hooked in his boxers, his brown eyes met hers. "Lena, you're still dressed."

"Uh-huh." She picked the toy cuffs off the bed. Out of the corner of her eye, she saw his boxers hit the floor. "Hands behind your back, Chad."

He obeyed, positioning his wrists by his low back, every delicious inch of him on full display.

"And here I thought I was on my best behavior at dinner," he murmured as she snapped the cuffs into place.

She ran her hands over his butt. "You were."

"This is my reward?" She could hear the wanting in his voice. "Not much of one if you're still dressed."

Her front still to his back, she unzipped her dress, allowing the material to pool at her feet. Adding her underwear to the pile, she said, "Is this better?"

Lena pressed her body against his, her lips and teeth grazing his shoulder.

"You're killing me," he growled. "Move around where I can see you."

With one hand on him, she traced the hard, muscular planes of his body. One glimpse at the raw need in his brown eyes and she knew that whatever happened tomorrow, she wanted tonight.

Sinking to her knees, Lena wrapped her hand around his cock. Her tongue licked the tip once and she drew back.

"Lena, I'm one minute away from begging you to release me. I'm dying to run my fingers through your hair and push between your sweet lips."

"I'm not letting you go just yet," she murmured, running her hand up from the base to the tip. "Let's see how long these handcuffs last."

CHAD TILTED HIS head back, studying the motel room ceiling. One look at the gorgeous, naked woman on her knees in front of him and he'd lose it.

"Lena." His voice was low and rough. "I'm pretty damn close to begging."

Finally, she wrapped her lips around him, taking him deep. He let her set the pace, her hand stroking him, rising up to meet her lips, as he stared down at her.

Beautiful, sexy, strong—even if she didn't feel it now—this woman made him question his wants, his needs, his plans for the future . . . everything. She made him want to be better, to transform their fake relationship into something tangible. Because from where he was standing, they'd already crossed that line. Hadn't they?

She released his cock, placing her hands on his thighs as she stood, her palms running up over his hips, his abs, stopping at his chest.

"I'm tempted to climb up," she said, rising to her tiptoes, her lips nearly touching his ear. "Wrap my legs tight around you, and ride you long and hard."

Hell, the way she turned the tables . . .

"I freaking love it when you whisper naughty things in my ear," he said. "Now go lie down on the bed. It's my turn to touch you, taste you, and make you scream."

She raised an eyebrow, but she followed orders. Lying on the bed, she spread her legs and arched her back. The view ratcheted the tension pulsing through him to an eleven on a scale of one to ten.

"Lena." He pulled at the plastic restraints. "Another night I swear I'll lick you, burying my tongue inside you until you call my name. Tonight I need you, beautiful. No more teasing. No more foreplay."

The plastic "chain" holding his wrists together snapped. With his hands free, he retrieved his wallet from his pants pocket and pulled out the condom he'd stashed there earlier. He tore open the wrapper, quickly covering himself before approaching the bed.

"I'm not going to lie, Lena. I want you hard and fast. I want you on your knees, your ass in the air, my hands on your hips, holding you tight as I bury my cock inside you."

"I've never liked lies," she murmured, rolling onto her stomach. She rose off the mattress on her hands and knees. "Like this?"

"Yes," he growled. "Yes."

He moved to the edge of the bed, teasing her entrance with the head of his cock, one hand running over her low back, exploring her curves.

"Just like that." He thrust inside her and she cried out, pressing back against him. His palms moved over her backside, one settling at her waist, and the other moving higher toward the long locks he'd fantasized about pulling from that first night in the studio over the barn.

"Chad." His name was like a plea, a cry for more. "Chad, please."

Quickening the pace, he thrust into her again and again, the physical pleasure rising with each movement.

"I want you to come with me," he said.

"Yes," she murmured.

His hand wrapped around the long strands of hair cascading down her back and pulled. Her head drawn back, her blue eyes stared into his, the wild, wanton look matching the need pulsing through him to claim her. But in that instant, his cock buried deep inside her, his hold on her a potent mixture of command and possession, Chad realized his mistake.

He should have tossed the cheap handcuffs in the trash, come in here and made love to her. In this moment, she was his, but it was fleeting. Tomorrow, he vowed as his climax pushed aside the doubts. Tomorrow he'd make love to her. No toys or games. He felt her tighten around him, heard her scream his name, and then he was lost.

Still panting, they shifted their bodies, maneuvering under the sheets side by side. He rolled away from her only for a moment to discard the condom.

"Are you hungry?" he asked. "We still have that Chinese food."

"No," she murmured. "Save it for breakfast."

He laughed, wrapping his arms around her, drawing her back against his front. But even with the soft contours of her curves pressed against him, there was a gap he could not close. She was *his*, dammit. The first woman who'd forced him to open his eyes to the possibility of more.

But the words "temporary" and "fake" still hung over their heads, provided a buffer he didn't want or need. He hoped she'd felt the same because tomorrow he planned to lock those words in the past.

"Chad?" she whispered.

"Yeah?"

"Thank you—"

"You don't need to thank me, Lena. I was right there with you." He hugged her tight.

"Being with you," she said. "I feel one step closer to normal. I feel like maybe I can face tomorrow's ceremony."

"You can." He kissed her neck, debating whether to tell her about his conversation with the sergeant in charge of the event. But now when she was drifting off to sleep wasn't the time. And part of him wanted to surprise her.

"I know you can," he added.

And after the vice president handed her the Silver Star, after they put the ceremony behind them, they'd have eight hours in the car to find new words to define their relationship.

Chapter 18

LENA FOLDED HER hands in her lap, staring straight ahead while Chad handed over their IDs and the vehicle registration. Wearing her dress uniform for the first time in more months than she wished to count, with her hair pulled into a tight bun, she felt an eerie calm.

"Have you been here before?" Chad asked as he pulled away from the checkpoint.

"No. I was stationed in Virginia." She glanced at the window as they drove past a cluster of buildings. Men and women, some in uniform and others in civilian clothes, walked along the paved pathways. "But it feels familiar."

There were days when she still missed the precision of military life. The need to survey her surroundings haunted her in Oregon, but while deployed, while doing her job, it had been a necessary part of life.

"Being here, it does make me wonder if I should go back," she said.

"And give up normal?" Chad shook his head. "Don't tell me you were lying last night when you said I'd brought you one step closer."

"I was telling the truth, Chad. What you've done for me—"

"Give yourself some credit, beautiful. It takes two to do what we did last night."

"Too bad orgasms aren't the cure-all to PTSD."

Chad laughed, steering them away from the main buildings. "Yeah, I think the VA might be bombarded with claims."

"Chad." She glanced down at the map of the base with the red arrow pointing to the locale of the ceremony. "I think you're going the wrong way."

"Nope, I spoke with the sergeant in charge last night. They changed the location," he said, pulling up in front of a one-story office building. "There's a conference room inside that will work for today."

"They moved the ceremony from an auditorium to a conference room? Did the vice president cancel?"

"No." Cutting the engine, he faced her. "But I told them you would unless it was friends and family only. No press, no surprises. And if the vice president gets too close, have Hero give him a shove. This is your day, Lena."

She drew a shaky breath, and her eyes filled with unshed tears.

"Nope, no crying." He opened his door and hopped down. "I pissed off a lot of people last night, especially the woman who'd planned this thing. So try to look happy about the change."

He held the door as she stepped down. "Chad Summers, you're full of surprises. I never would have guessed you'd be the one to ride in and save the day."

He raised one eyebrow. "Confusing me with your dog again? I'm not your hero, Lena. I'm your friend. And yeah, I care a helluva lot about you. But that's something we can talk about later. Right now, I need to give you this."

He held out a folded piece of paper. Plucking it from his fingers, she started to open it.

Chad's hand covered hers. "Not yet. Save it for later. Just in case things get a little tense in there and you need something to make you smile."

"Thank you." She formed a tight fist around the note.

"Now, let's go get your medal," Chad said. "Ready?"

She nodded, taking Chad's hand. Inside, they walked down the hall past a row of cubicles toward the conference room. Dressed for the occasion in his service dog vest, Hero marched by her side. She'd left his chew toy in the car and she could have sworn he was pouting. Or maybe he sensed her rising nerves.

Lena paused in the open doorway to the conference room. Her parents and Joe sat at one end of the oval table. Both her father and brother had worn their dress uniforms. A few unfamiliar faces moved about the space, one held a large camera. She continued to scan the room, taking in every detail. Windows with the shades drawn lined one wall. A small table stood at the far end of the room with a box on it. The Silver Star. Her medal. If she stepped into the space.

Lena drew her lower lip between her teeth and her feet remained planted to the ground. It looked safe, but there were so many people even in this smaller venue. And she would never be able to keep an eye on every corner of the room while standing beside the table. Someone could move behind her.

A man in suit, wearing an earpiece that suggested he belonged to the vice president's Secret Service detail, rushed into the room. Her breath caught and her hands went numb. The man moved quickly as if running away from something.

A loud crash sounded and she jumped. She had to get out of here. Run. Take cover. It wasn't safe. At her feet, Hero barked and spun in circles, demanding her attention. She glanced down at him and felt the panic recede. But not far enough. Not this time.

She stepped back, her breath coming in short, desperate gasps. *Not enough oxygen.* The word flashed through her mind like a warning.

"Lena?" Chad said. "What's wrong?"

"I can't." Her voice shook with the fear. She pulled her hand free from his, feeling the terror take hold. "I can't . . . I can't breathe."

Oh God, she would suffocate, right here, with all these people watching, if she didn't run. Feeling as if she was dragging her feet through quicksand, she spun around and headed for the door with Hero at her heels.

In the parking lot, she ran to the truck, pulling on the passenger side door. Locked, dammit. She stumbled to the back of the pickup and scrambled inside. Her vision blurred as she collapsed onto her back. Closing her eyes, she tried to breathe.

A weight covered her chest and a wet nose touched her ear. Hero. He'd followed her. And with his reassuring presence covering her, keeping her safe, the panic slowly faded. Sweat ran down her face. She could feel the sting in her eyes. But the worst was over. Oxygen flowed through her body again and feeling returned to her limbs.

In her hand, she felt the crumpled piece of paper. Maneuvering her arms around Hero, she lifted her hand and unfolded the note.

When you're screaming my name, I don't give a damn if you have a Silver Star or not. I'd rather see you stripped down, your legs spread, your fingers exploring the places I'm dying to taste. I want to run a trail of kisses over you . . .

Are you blushing yet?

Scanning the naughty words, she could hear his voice in her head, offering instructions, making demands. Maybe if she'd entered the room, she could have accepted the Silver Star, opening his note when panic threatened, and she felt her cheeks warm.

Instead, she'd run.

Her hands dropped to her sides as her eyes squeezed shut. Clutching the note in her hand, she let the tears flow.

Running away from a Silver Star, her family, and the man who cared enough to make demands from the army proved one thing. She had derailed on her road to normal. She still was too broken.

Chapter 19

CHAD WANTED TO tear to pieces the fucking idiot who'd tripped over the tripod. Dammit, he wanted this moment for her. She deserved to receive that medal. He'd tried everything he could think of to make it work, but it wasn't enough.

Without a backward glance at her family, or the other people filling the small room, he turned and sprinted for the door. Maybe he couldn't make this ceremony possible, but he refused to let her fall apart alone. Scanning the parking area, Chad spotted Hero's tail in the bed of his pickup. Rounding the back, he heard the sobbing.

"Lena?" He froze. The sight inside the pickup's bed gutted him. Lena was on her back with Hero covering her chest. But even beneath the dog, her entire body shook as she wept.

"Lena, can I come up?" he asked, not sure of the rules right now.

"I need to leave." She drew a deep, shaky breath as she

pushed Hero off her body and sat up. "Please, Chad. I need to get away from here now."

"OK," he said. "OK. I'll going to lower the gate. Make it easier for you to climb out."

Keeping his moments slow and measured, he lowered it and held out his hand. But she shook her head as she moved toward him and hopped out on her own. Hero followed, hugging her side. The retriever studied Lena with a furrowed brow as if he knew the panic still lingered.

"Lena—"

"Just drive, Chad. Get me out of here." Lena moved to the passenger side and climbed in, allowing Hero to settle in her lap.

Feeling as if he was swimming upstream against a river of helplessness, his hopes for their future rushing past, flowing in the opposite direction, Chad followed her orders. Minutes later, they were on the road, leaving behind her family, the vice president, and everyone else involved with today's event.

A sick feeling settled in his gut as they drove in silence. The woman who'd claimed a part of him that he'd never planned to offer anyone felt so damn distant right now, so far beyond his reach, he wanted to scream in frustration. He knew she had her reasons and that they existed beyond her control, but that didn't erase the feeling that she was slipping farther and farther away from him with each mile marker they passed.

EIGHT PAINFULLY LONG hours later, the truck pulled up in front of the Summers family farmhouse. Finally, she could get this weight off her. Hero had insisted on spending the entire drive on her lap. Opening the passenger side door, Lena let her dog out before stepping down and stretching her legs.

"Lena." Chad stood in front of her, his hand in the pockets of the slacks he'd worn to the ceremony hours earlier. There was no sign of his trademark humor in his brown eyes. And it felt like years since she'd seen his smile. Her stomach flipped knowing they needed to talk about how she'd erased his grin with one epic panic attack.

She glanced at the door, wishing she could fast-forward and begin nursing her heartache. She wanted to escape inside and have a date with the bag of chocolate chips in her kitchenette. After this conversation, Lena had a feeling mouthwatering chocolate would be the closest she'd get to orgasm territory for a long time. And beyond the bedroom doors, she'd lose the one person who delivered passion, kindness, and hope into her life—the one man who believed in her.

"Lena, we need to talk," he said. "I didn't want to say anything on the ride."

Because he'd known this conversation would lead to a downward spiral and he wanted her to have the space to walk away and fall apart. At every turn, this man put her needs first. He'd convinced the army to rearrange a medal presentation featuring the vice president *for her.*

"But I need to know you're OK," he said.

"I'm not."

A wash of failure rushed over her, threatening to swallow her up. Turning away from Chad, she focused on the physical and mundane. She reached into the bed of his truck and retrieved her overnight bag. Their relationship had transformed into something real and tangible, something that demanded more than she had to give right now. What they shared—the wild nights in his bed, the laughter, the friendship that took her by surprise at every turn—it couldn't be more.

Running away had dissolved any hope of a future for them, proving she wasn't ready. Now, she had to say those words—"It's over"—and walk away. The realization tore into her, ripping her apart like a well-aimed bullet. She'd felt invincible on the battlefield, racing through enemy fire to save her fellow soldiers. But now, an ocean away from the gunfire, she felt as if she'd been hit. She might not be able to save herself. But she could still save him.

"Lena." His brow furrowed and he took a step toward her, his arms outstretched. Instinct demanded she step back, and Hero quickly moved between them, forming a barrier. After weeks together, they were back where they'd started. She was broken, lost on her road to normal. And he was out of reach.

"I'm sorry," she added, hating those words with a fierce and rising passion. How many more times would she need to apologize for emotions and reactions that stemmed from feelings beyond her control? If she stayed, if she kept trying to be with him, those words would likely become her constant refrain. She would never be enough for him.

Lena closed her eyes. Her mind ticked off the things she'd miss—his panty-melting grin, the way he made her laugh, the way he supported her without demanding results . . .

Opening her eyes, she drew in a deep, shaky breath, and an ugly hiccup escaped. Tears welled in her eyes. One escaped, rolling down her cheek.

"You went to so much trouble to rearrange the ceremony," she said.

"Lena, I don't give a damn about the medal. I didn't want you to be afraid."

"But I panicked." Another hiccup punctuated her sentence. "I thought I was getting closer . . ."

"There's no timetable," he insisted, staring into her watery eyes. "Take all the time you need."

"Chad, please. I can't." Her voice trembled. "I think we should end our deal."

"What we have is real, Lena. There is nothing fake about what I feel for you."

"I know," she said. "Which is why we need to walk away now."

"No. Lena—"

"You deserve more than I have to give right now. You have so much to offer, Chad. So much. But I'm not ready to accept it." She offered a sad smile, fighting back the tears. "I'm just glad we got you up in the air, flying, and doing what you love."

"Shit, Lena, this isn't about flying a damn helicopter." He raised his hands, running them through his hair as he glanced down at her dog in frustration. But Hero didn't give an inch, refusing to allow Chad closer to her.

"I care about you," he added.

"But if I stay, and you wait for me to get better . . . I'm just so afraid I'll disappoint you too. And the thought of adding another failure to my long list, I can't do it. You've done so much for me. But now I need to stand on my own. I need to find my own place. Move out of here."

"Jesus, Lena, you don't have to leave the apartment—"

"I'll find a new apartment this week." She picked up her bag and turned to the door leading up to her borrowed home. Hero abandoned his post and moved to her side. Maybe she could find four walls and a roof to rent this week, but her own place? She still felt too far adrift right now, too lost.

"Good-bye, Chad."

"Lena, wait," he called.

She froze, glancing over her shoulder. Hero sat at her side glancing back at Chad and then at her with his head cocked, a pleading look in his dark eyes, which she swore said, *Are you sure you don't want to bring him? I kinda like him.*

"For the record, you never disappointed me or let me down," he said. "Not once."

Chapter 20

Chad headed for his truck, bone-tired from flying since dawn. Lying awake half the night every night for the past week, thinking about Lena, hating the fact that she'd moved out and away from him, hadn't helped. Pulling away from the landing site, he glanced at his helicopter.

This was it. His dream. But it felt more like a nightmare. Yeah, he was living the life he'd always wanted—single and flying. And it broke his heart every damn day.

In his pocket, his cell vibrated. Chad pulled over to the side of the dirt road and took the call, hoping to hear her voice.

"Chad here."

"Hey." Brody's deep voice filled his ear, and disappointment surged. "I need you to swing by the rehab center and check on Josh."

Pinning the phone between his shoulder and ear, Chad

put the truck in gear and headed for the main road. "Everything OK?"

"One of the nurses called. They're worried he's slipping into depression. There's been no change in weeks."

"Yeah, and that last specialist was a total loss." The doctor from Seattle had tossed up his hands and said there was nothing he could do. "What should I tell him?"

"If he asks, say we're working on it. I have a list of doctors to interview this week," his big brother said. "I'm going to need your help with that."

"You got it. Whatever you need."

"Good. And try to keep the kid distracted. Talk about something else. Anything to take his mind off his missing memory."

"Will do." Chad ended the call and merged onto the highway heading for the university rehab center. Forty-five minutes later, he parked his truck, went inside, and found Josh lying on his bed staring at the ceiling.

"Hey man, you got a minute," Chad called from the doorway.

Josh laughed, sitting up. "Yeah, I got a few before, you know, bingo tonight or whatever shit they've got planned."

The bandages were gone from his head, and from the outside, his little brother looked perfectly normal. But Chad knew appearances could be deceiving.

"Good, I need to talk. It's about a girl."

"Don't tell me you need me to fix your love life."

"Yeah. I do." Chad sank into the chair by the window. Starting at the beginning, he told Josh about Lena. He explained their plan for the fake relationship, and how for him it turned real. Head leaned back, he closed his eyes and told the one person who wouldn't remember a word of this after bingo how he'd lost his heart to a woman who felt he deserved more.

"I fell for her, man. Hard." Chad opened his eyes and glanced over at the bed. "What the hell? Are you taking notes?"

Josh nodded, his focus on the pen and spiral notebook in his hands. "One of the nurses suggested it, so I remember."

"Shit, I told you because I thought you'd forget by dinner, not make a written account."

His little brother grinned. "Yeah, I know. But now I have something to hold over your head when I ask you to break me out of here."

"I can't do that. But—" Chad made a grab for the notebook, but his little brother held it out of his reach. "What do you think I should do?"

"If you care about her, don't let her go."

"She's already walked away from me once," Chad said.

"Then go after her. You might be flying a helicopter like Dad dreamed about doing, but you're not living his life. If you want her, go get her."

"You're right," Chad said with a heavy sigh. "And I wish it were that simple. But I know her, Josh. She needs space. Too many people in her life have made demands and set expectations that she couldn't meet."

"You can't just give up. Life's too short. Trust me, it could all slip away and you wouldn't remember it tomorrow." Josh sounded a helluva lot wiser than a twenty-seven-year-old should when it came to escaping death. "Isn't there something you could do?"

Chad stared at his brother's notebook. "I need to borrow that."

"I'll hide it under my pillow. No one will ever know about our little chat."

"And you'll forget about it." Chad held out his hand.

Josh gave in, handing it over. Flipping to a blank page in the back, Chad started writing.

"You're writing her a love letter?"

"Something like that."

"What the hell? Have you spent the past week drowning your broken heart in ice cream and romantic comedies?"

Chad ignored his brother and focused on the words. Getting it to her might prove challenging. She hadn't left a forwarding address. But he could enlist his sister's help. After reading through the note, he tore out the page, followed by the ones with Josh's notes about his love life, and handed it back to his brother.

"Thanks, bro." Chad turned to the door. "And have fun at bingo tonight."

"Yeah, it will be a blast," Josh said, not bothering to mask his sarcasm. "Hey, Chad?"

He paused in the doorway. "Yeah?"

"You're still looking, right?" His little brother's voice trembled slightly as if he was afraid to ask. "For a doctor who can fix me?"

"Yeah, we're on it. Brody's determined to find the right doctor. You and I both know he's never let us down. If Brody says he's going to find help, he will. And if he even thinks about giving up, I'll kick his ass. I'm not going to let you down."

Chapter 21

LENA MADE IT eight days, working, sleeping, and bingeing on chocolate, before Georgia found her in the Independence Falls grocery store, trying to decide between a Hershey's bar and bread. She couldn't afford both and still have enough for the rent on her new studio apartment.

Her parents had sent her a check along with the Silver Star they'd accepted on her behalf, and a note apologizing for failing her. After reading their heartfelt words, she'd swallowed her foolish pride and cashed the check. But it had barely covered the security deposit on her new place. She still needed to come up with the rental payments each month, which right now meant making hard choices—bread or chocolate.

"I need you to come over." Georgia tossed the chocolate bar into her cart filled with juice boxes, Cheerios, and bacon. "I'm finalizing a date, a venue, and shoes."

"What happened to the backyard wedding?" Lena placed the bread in her basket.

"Eric and I agreed that we didn't need to rush on account of his company's logging schedule. Liam can take over for him while we're getting married and away on our honeymoon. Plus we couldn't take a honeymoon over Christmas. Nate would be heartbroken. And the dress I found last weekend in Portland? They need a couple of months to order it. We're looking at an early spring date again."

Of course, it all came down to a dress, even for a woman who'd worn the same uniform day after day in a war zone. Or maybe especially for someone like Georgia, who'd missed fashion while serving halfway around the world.

"Katie plans to leave work a little early and come over. And Eric is taking Nate for a boys' adventure, a little early birthday celebration before his party on Saturday. We could sit on the patio and open a bottle of wine." Georgia held up the Hershey's bar. "Maybe some chocolate."

"I'm in," Lena said, following Georgia to the checkout with Hero at her side. "I'll follow you in my truck."

A half hour later, Lena settled into a lounge chair beside an outdoor heating tower. In her hands, she held the promised chocolate. Hero curled up at her feet. Not long ago, when she'd first moved to Independence Falls and the weather had been warmer, she'd sat here with Katie talking about boys. Now Katie was planning to build a home with the man she loved, Georgia was getting married—and Lena had walked away from the first man who'd made her believe that she was ready to open her heart and her life again.

"I booked Willamette Views Vineyard for the first weekend in April," Georgia announced, setting three shoe boxes on the patio. "Katie helped me pick out a dress. Now I need shoes. I'm thinking blue heels."

Georgia held up the first pair.

"Wow," Lena said. "Those are bright."

"April is a long time to wait." Katie filled her wineglass from the bottle they'd brought out to the patio. "What happened to December?"

"The dress," Lena said.

Katie smiled. "It gives me more time to plan the bachelorette."

"The coed backyard barbecue, right?" Georgia sank into a chair beside Katie, accepting a glass of wine. "No surprises. And no goats."

Katie laughed. "No livestock. But don't be surprised if you're not the first one down the aisle."

"Liam proposed?" Georgia said, her brown eyes widening. "My brother asked you to marry him?"

"No, but we've been talking about running away to Vegas for the weekend and just doing it."

"We're coming too. And your brothers." Georgia turned to her. "Don't tell me you and Chad are secretly planning to elope too. Another trip to city hall maybe?"

"No." Lena lowered the chocolate bar. "We ended things. About a week ago."

"That explains why my brother promised to clean the horse stalls for a week if I delivered a note to you." Katie set her wineglass on the blue stone patio and reached for her purse, withdrawing a small folded piece of paper. "I was so excited to hear about the wedding plans I almost forgot."

Katie handed the piece of paper to Lena, adding, "I was tempted to peek inside, but I didn't. Promise."

"Chad sent you another love note?" Georgia said. "I always thought you brought out the best in him."

"Another?" Katie reclaimed her wineglass.

Lena unfolded the paper, her focus on the words, not Georgia's explanation of the gas receipt note she'd delivered at the gun range.

You're not the only one who doesn't give up. Maybe you don't feel ready now. But when you are, I'll be waiting. And the rules stand. I've always respected your boundaries and I always will. Take the time you need. Find your strength. Your kisses, your heart, and your love—I'd wait forever for those, beautiful.

She stared at the paper, reading the words a second time. After she'd walked out of his life, he still refused to give up on her. He continued to offer her the time and space she needed to heal.

"But I don't want to wait," she murmured.

"Wait for what?" Georgia asked.

Lena looked up at her friends. "Chad. He said he'd wait until I felt ready for us. To be part of an 'us.' But I don't want to wait."

Chad helped her every step of the way. He'd witnessed

her bone-deep need to succeed, to find her way forward—and he'd helped her get there. She'd bargained for a physical relationship, at night, when they were alone. But he'd given her so much more.

He'd opened her eyes, with his charming smile, his sexy notes, and his humor, and made her see that every little moment of panic was not a sign of failure. It was part of who she was now.

"At the medal ceremony, I let my fear win," she said, forcing herself to face the raw truth. "I was afraid I wasn't enough for him—"

"Georgia!" Eric Moore's voice boomed from the sliding doorway.

Lena dropped the note, the words "but maybe I am" frozen on her tongue. Together, the three of them stood, focusing on Eric's serious expression.

Oh no, Lena thought as his gaze settled on Katie.

"Georgia, I need you to stay with Nate," Eric said, his tone dead serious. "Katie, can you get ahold of Brody?"

Katie nodded, slipping her phone out of her pocket. "Is Josh OK?" she asked, her voice wavering.

"It's not Josh." Eric hesitated, his gaze moving from one woman to the next as if debating how much to tell them. "I got a call from the harvest site. They can't get the helicopter off the ground because someone is pointing a gun at the pilot."

Chapter 22

"Who is it?" Katie demanded. "Who's pointing a gun at my brother?"

"I don't know." Eric sped down the bumpy dirt road, both hands on the steering wheel of his company truck, his cell phone pinned between his shoulder and ear. "I'm on the line with Liam trying to find out."

"Liam's there?" Lena heard the panic in Katie's voice. "Oh God, what if this lunatic shoots him too?"

Eric tossed the phone on the dash and sped up. "It's Tim. Liam confirmed the shooter is my former crew chief, dammit. I fired him a few weeks ago after he showed up high to a job site. I told him it was the last straw, that I'd heard he'd been stoned off his ass at the pizza place not long before that and I didn't want anyone in town wondering if I let someone use a chainsaw in his condition."

"He blames Chad for losing his job?" Katie said. "That's

ridiculous. Half the town saw him there that night. And that was over a month ago."

"Liam thinks Tim's under the influence right now. Drunk, stoned—we don't know. According to Liam, Tim showed up waving a piece of paper, screaming about paying his mortgage, and then pulled a gun. Tim's looking for someone to blame and he came up with the guy who threatened him at the pizza place."

"How close are we?" Lena asked from the backseat. With one arm wrapped around Hero, she reached her free hand into her purse, needing to feel her gun. She knew the power of a single bullet. She'd witnessed the damage one shot could do to a person, cutting off the possibility of a future. And when it came to guns and crazy people, every second counted.

"Can you drive faster?" she demanded.

"We're close," Eric said, making a sharp left turn into a dense forest. "One minute to the landing."

He put his cell down. "When we get there, I need you ladies to stay in the car."

"No." Lena withdrew the revolver from her bag as Eric put the truck in park. "Hero stays here, but I'm coming with you."

"Lena." He glanced back and spotted the gun in her hand.

"I'm coming with you," she repeated, pushing the seat forward and following Katie out the passenger side of the truck.

Katie ran to Liam, wrapping her body around him. Running a hand over her hair, his arm banded tight around his girlfriend's waist, Liam glared at Eric. "You brought her here?"

"I couldn't keep her away."

"Katie, honey, it's not safe," Liam said. "I need you to wait in the truck."

"No. Where's Chad?" Katie demanded. "Where's my brother?"

Lena scanned the clearing, spotted the twin rotor helicopter resting on the field. Five feet in front, Chad stood with his hands raised over his head, his brown eyes focused on the man with the hunting rifle.

Determination swelled, leaving no room for panic. She'd trained for years to take out the enemy. Right now, the man staring down the barrel of the shotgun at Chad was her number one adversary. And unlike the anxiety that followed her around day and night, she could take this one out with a single shot. She could do this. Her arms raised, Lena marched across the clearing, the revolver aimed at the target with a laserlike focus.

"Tim, put the gun down," she ordered.

Out of the corner of her eye, she saw Chad's jaw tighten. But Lena kept her gaze focused on the wild-eyed man who looked like he'd walked out of her nightmares and into her life, her fingers ready to pull the trigger. But this wasn't a dream. And if she wanted something real with the man standing in front of the helicopter, she needed to fight for it. Now. Falling apart was not an option.

The Silver Star in a box under her bed wasn't worth much to her. But Chad? He was everything. And she wasn't about to let some jerk with a shotgun steal her chance to tell him.

Or a panic attack, dammit. She had to hold the fear at bay until she'd removed the threat.

"Lena," Chad said, through clenched teeth. "Get back in the truck. Now."

"I'm sorry, Chad. I never thought standing up for me over pizza would end with another gun pointed at you," she said, forcing her voice to remain calm and her focus on the man with the weapon.

"We've called the police," Eric said. "They're on their way now. You need to put the gun down, Tim. I know you're upset, man, but this solves nothing."

Lena saw the sweat on Tim's brow. He was nervous, jumpy, and likely to do something stupid. She had a feeling waiting for the police was not an option.

"How the hell am I supposed to pay my mortgage now?" Tim demanded, moving his arms just enough with each word that her instincts screamed, *Take him out*, but her mind knew to wait for a clear shot.

"You told Eric I was high and I scared your crazy girlfriend who is afraid of her damn shadow," Tim continued.

"Do I looked scared right now, Tim?" she called, drawing his attention away from Chad, hoping he'd aim his weapon at her—and offer a clear path for a bullet. She only had one shot at this. If she failed, he'd fire on Chad.

"Because you don't frighten me," she added, feeling the truth of those words down to her fingertips. She had a mountain of fears, including losing Chad before she had a chance to talk to him. Tim didn't make the list.

But the intoxicated man with the shotgun ignored her, focusing on Chad. "Eric never would have accused me if you hadn't gone and tattled like a little girl."

"He wasn't the only one who saw you," Eric said. "Put the gun down and we'll talk about it."

With a flick of his thumb, Tim removed the safety. "No."

Lena focused on her breath. Her finger slipped into position on an inhale, preparing to shoot as the measured breath left her body. She refused to lose Chad when she'd finally realized that the one thing she had to offer him—love—might be enough.

Staring down the barrel of her revolver, Lena exhaled and pulled the trigger.

Chapter 23

The shot rang out and Chad ran toward the noise. Lena. He saw a swirl of color, her long dress billowing as she raced forward. Relief mixed with adrenaline, but he kept moving, chasing after her. He reached her side as she slid Tim's gun out away from his bleeding hand.

"Nice shot," Chad said.

"There are some things I'm very good at, and this is one of them," she said, her gaze focused on the wounded man at her feet. "I couldn't let him shoot you."

"Yeah, I feel the same about you. I was terrified he'd turn his rifle and aim it at you." Chad looped his arm around her waist. "Maybe I should start carrying a gun."

"I think your skills lie elsewhere," she murmured.

Police sirens echoed through the forest, the sound drawing closer and closer to the clearing. Eric, Liam, and Katie joined them, forming a semicircle around the cursing, bleeding man on the ground. Katie threw her arms around his neck, hugging him tight as he kept his hold on Lena.

"I'm glad you're OK," Katie said. "I couldn't handle two brothers in the hospital."

Chad released his sister. "Thank Lena. She's the one who shot him."

If she hadn't fired first . . . no, he couldn't let his mind go there. Lena was a warrior. He believed in her.

Medics rushed over, lifting the pale-faced Tim onto the stretcher. Police officers, led by Rick Maxwell, a guy who'd graduated high school with Brody, led the pack.

"She shot my fucking hand! She's crazy," Tim whimpered as the medics wheeled the stretcher toward the waiting ambulance.

"Here is the weapon." Lena handed her revolver to Rick.

"It was self-defense," Chad added.

Rick slipped Lena's gun into an evidence bag, handed it off to another man in uniform before crouching down beside Tim's gun. Picking up the unfired weapon, he looked up at the small crowd gathered. "I'm going to need statements from everyone."

"Yes, sir," Lena said as Chad wrapped an arm around her. Holding her close, he could feel her breathing shift as she drew air in short gasps. It was as if letting go of her weapon had opened the door to panic. Over the noise at the scene, he heard barking.

"Katie," Chad said. "Get Hero. Now."

With Liam at her side, Katie ran to the Moore Timber truck, opened the door, and released the frantic golden retriever. Hero raced to his owner, jumping up, pushing her out of Chad's arms and onto the ground. The dog lay across her chest, his nose beside her cheek.

"He's a service dog," Chad explained to the officers. "Lena served in the army."

Rick nodded. "We'll still need your statements, but I can start with someone else. Just let me know when you're ready."

Eric clapped Rick on the shoulder. "I'll start."

HOURS LATER, THE trucks and police cruisers pulled away from the landing site. The sun had slipped behind the mountains, while Rick and his team had done their job, taking statements from everyone who'd been working at the site and seen the events unfold. The officer in charge had agreed with Chad—self-defense.

Lena climbed into Chad's truck, sliding across the bench and leaving the window for Hero. Chad claimed the driver's seat and turned on the truck. Headlights illuminated the helicopter sitting in the middle of the clearing. A physical reminder of what had led them down this path—the common belief that dreams were worth fighting for, even if they seemed silly or small, like surviving the day, or finding a job.

"Chad." She needed to say this now, before they drove away from this place. "I read your note. Before all of this started. And I realized that by walking away I'd marched headfirst into failure. Even if I struggle every day to get back to a normal life, I don't want it to stop me from loving you. I don't want to let the fear win. You deserve more—"

"More than a woman who saves my life?" He took her hand, interlacing their fingers as he turned to face her. "Lena, I think you're the only person out there who would shoot a nut job with a hunting rifle for me."

She glanced down at their joined hands as pride swelled. Maybe she couldn't accept a medal in a cramped, crowded conference room, but when he needed her, she could step up. And it didn't matter that she fallen apart afterward, her dog pinning her to the ground, because she'd saved him.

"I made a mistake too," Chad continued. "I've spent my whole adult life hiding from heartache, scared I'm going to end up like my dad, watching the door slam behind the woman I love, that I never stopped to think that finding the right woman is worth the risk. Seeing you out there today, knowing a madman might turn his gun on you . . . Shit, I think today proved that I'm not a guy who rushes in and saves the day. If anyone is lacking here, it's me."

She placed her hand on his cheek. "I don't need the strongest man, or the one who is the best shot. I don't need you to save me from crazy, stupid, stoned idiots. I need the man who makes me laugh, whose wicked words leave me craving his touch—"

"I can be your hero at night, Lena. That I can do." He ran the back of his hand over her cheek. "But—"

"No 'buts,' " she ordered. "Listen to me, Chad. I need the man who believes in me. I have a long road ahead of me littered with nightmares, and horrible rushes of anxiety that I can't control. I want the man who believes those things don't hold me back, even when I can't believe it myself."

She rested her forehead against his. "You're my hero, Chad, and not only at night. Just by being you."

Alone in the quiet truck, Hero's breathing the only sound, she let her words sink in before adding the ones she'd been waiting to say to him.

"I love you." She brushed her lips over his. "Chad Summers, I love you just the way you are."

He kissed her back, claiming her mouth. Melting into him, she savored the intimate touch. She let out a soft moan, protesting as he stole his lips away from hers. His mouth hovering close to hers, as he said the words she'd been waiting to hear.

"I love you too, beautiful."

Epilogue

Five months later . . .

Brody weaved through the parked cars and pickups searching for the one with the windows fogged up, and the golden retriever standing guard by the passenger side door. Behind him, the party was in full swing celebrating Georgia and Eric. In forty-eight hours, the head of Moore Timber and his girl would walk down the aisle. Brody had no doubt that every detail would be flawless, just like the coed bachelorette/bachelor party his little sister had spent the past six months or so planning. And he would be there to witness the big event—if he made it back in time.

Hero barked and Brody followed the sound to the Chad's truck. Raising his hand, he knocked on the window. "Chad," he called.

Brody heard scrambling. The horn honked. He closed

his eyes, shaking his head. Standing here, waiting for his little brother to stop whatever he'd been doing in the truck—and Brody had a pretty good idea even if it had been too damn long since he'd met a woman he could take to bed—he felt old.

The driver's side opened and Chad slipped out, careful to close the door behind him. His little brother's flannel shirt was unbuttoned, but at least Chad had his pants on.

"You're missing the party," Brody said, crossing his arms in front of his chest.

Chad raised an eyebrow. "You came out here to drag me back?"

"No," Brody said with a heavy sign. "I need to go. A call came in. A group of hikers are lost on Mount Hood."

Chad shook his head. "You don't need to take every call. They have search and rescue volunteers in Portland. Take some downtime. You just got back from a rescue."

"They need more hands on this one. Some of the hikers are kids. They need all the help they can get."

"You'll be back for the wedding?"

"Yeah, I should. I'm picking up the new doctor, the woman from New York that you interviewed last week, on Saturday morning. But I should be back for the wedding."

"Good." Chad grinned. "Maybe you'll meet someone. I can ask Lena if there are any single ladies on the guest list."

"Don't even think about setting me up." Brody backed away. "I told Eric I had to take off, but do me a favor before the rehearsal dinner tomorrow and check on Josh."

"Done. And Brody?"

"Yeah?"

"Be safe out there."

Brody nodded. "Always."

CHAD WAITED UNTIL his big brother disappeared from sight. He was tempted to sit Brody down and have a long talk with him about what was important in life. Work and duty were on the list, but not at the top. In Chad's book, love came first, or at least it did now that he had Lena in his life.

But he had a feeling his big brother wouldn't listen. He'd been caring for others for so long, he'd forgotten how to take a break and do something for himself—like get laid.

"Don't tell me you got dressed," Chad said, slipping into the truck once the coast was clear, careful to keep Hero on the outside.

"No, I'm still ready and waiting for you," Lena murmured, pulling him close for a kiss as her hands pushed his shirt off his shoulders.

With his mouth pressed against hers, he unbuttoned his pants, and with her help slid them down over his hips.

"We're acting like teenagers," Lena murmured, sliding onto Chad's lap, her back to the steering wheel. "We should rejoin the party."

"Soon, beautiful. First I need to hear you scream my name."

Lena rocked her hips against him, letting him feel how wet and ready she was for him. In one fluid motion, she reached over, plucked a condom off the dash, and covered him. Holding his cock with one hand, she took him in, inch by inch.

They rocked together, allowing the pleasure to build. They had all night to make love. And the next night and the night after that . . .

Chad cupped her bare breasts, teasing her nipples, his gaze fixed on her face. This was not the time or the place, but the words slipped out anyway. "Ever think about getting married again?"

Lena stilled above him, her body tightening its hold on his cock. "Chad Summers, are you proposing?"

"No, Lena." He ran his hands up to her collarbone and down over her arms. Wrapping his fingers around her wrists, he pinned them behind her back. "You'll know when I'm proposing. Right now, I'm just asking if you think about it."

"Look at me," she ordered.

He loved the way she vied for control while he held her tight. "Oh, I'm looking, beautiful."

"I love you, Chad Summers," she said, her blue eyes shining bright. "And I want to spend the rest of my life with you. So when you're ready, ask."

Hope swelled inside him. He didn't doubt her. He had faith in their love for each other. But he wanted more. He wanted her forever.

Releasing her wrists, he cupped her face in his hands, drawing her lips down to meet his. He kissed her softly, savoring the intimate touch.

"I will, Lena. Count on it."

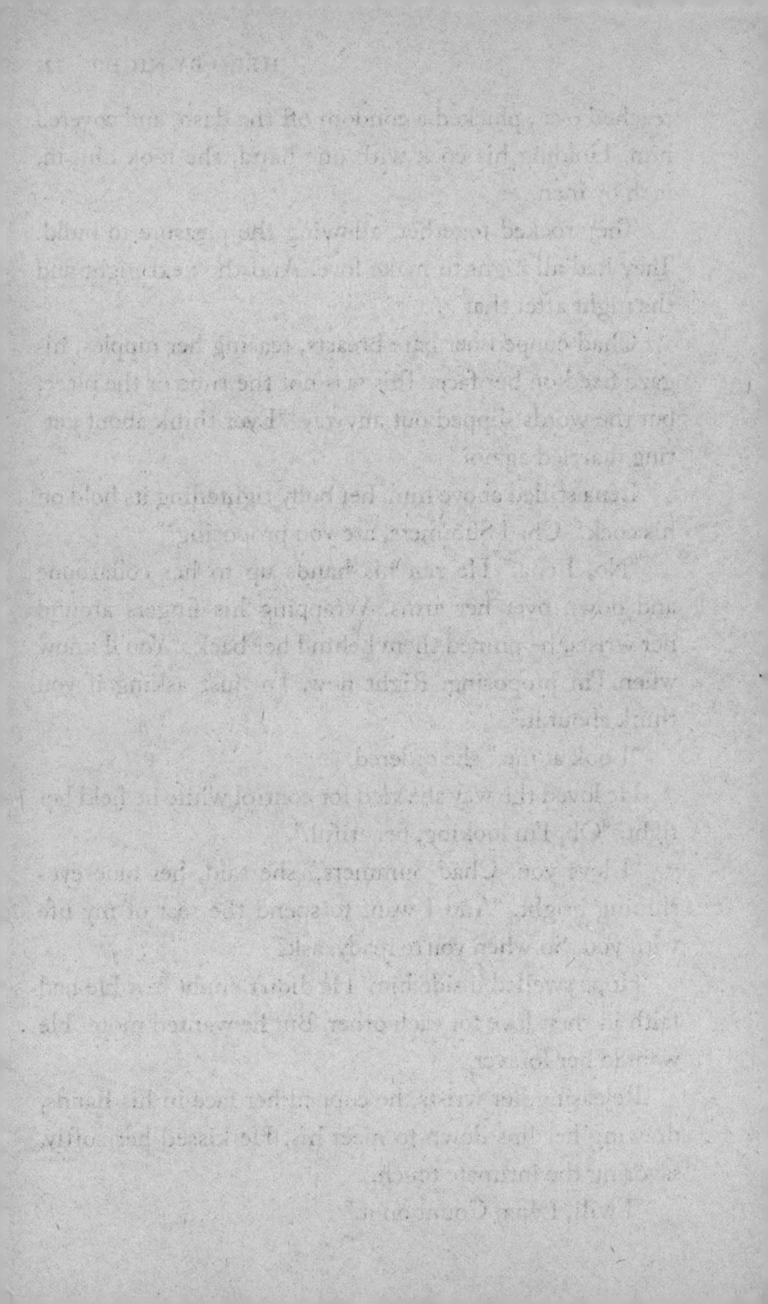

Coming April 2015

Wild With You

Book Four: Independence Falls

One night with a hero is just what she needs. But more spells trouble . . .

Growing up on the wrong side of everything, Dr. Katherine "Kat" Arnold left small-town life in Independence Falls for New York City and never looked back. But when she is asked to consult on a case involving a young man who lost his short-term memory following a logging accident, Kat relents. Part of her looks forward to showing her hometown how she has thrived. And she doesn't have to wait long. Her first night in Portland, before she drives to Independence Falls, she sees *him*. Tall, dark, and handsome, Brody Summers is a familiar face in a sea of strangers. But he doesn't connect her polished doctor persona with the girl who watched him from afar in high school. It seems like the perfect opportunity for a down-and-dirty affair with the man of her dreams . . .

Brody Summers saves people. For years, he looked out for his younger siblings and ran the family business. Now he works search and rescue. After a botched mission outside of Portland, Brody heads to the city, planning to take a night off. And he wouldn't say no to no-holds-barred sex with the blond city girl. But the next day when he returns to his duties as head of the family and meets his brother's new doctor, Brody realizes the past is returning to haunt him—and it goes back further than one wild night.

The last thing Kat wants is a reason to extend her stay in the town that failed her as a child. But she can't escape the memory of Brody's wicked touch, or the desire for more.

Brody is counting on Kat to help his brother. He can't allow their personal relationship, past or present, to interfere. But as the passion heats up, Brody wonders if he is falling for the one woman who doesn't need or want him to be her hero. And what would it take to change her mind?

About the Author

After several years on the other side of the publishing industry, SARA JANE STONE bid good-bye to her sales career to pursue her dream—writing romance novels. Sara Jane currently resides in Brooklyn, New York, with her very supportive real-life hero, two lively young children, and a lazy Burmese cat. Visit her online at www.sarajanestone.com or find her on Facebook at www.facebook.com/SaraJaneStone.

Join Sara Jane's newsletter to receive new release information, news about contests, giveaways, and more! To subscribe, visit www.sarajanestone.com and look for her newsletter entry form.

Give in to your impulses . . .
Read on for a sneak peek at seven brand-new e-book original tales of romance from Avon Impulse.
Available now wherever e-books are sold.

HOLDING HOLLY

A Love and Football Novella

By Julie Brannagh

IT'S A WONDERFUL FIREMAN

A Bachelor Firemen Novella

By Jennifer Bernard

ONCE UPON A HIGHLAND CHRISTMAS

By Lecia Cornwall

RUNNING HOT

A Bad Boys Undercover Novella

By HelenKay Dimon

SINFUL REWARDS 1

A Billionaires and Bikers Novella

By Cynthia Sax

RETURN TO CLAN SINCLAIR

A Clan Sinclair Novella

By Karen Ranney

RETURN OF THE BAD GIRL

By Codi Gary

An Excerpt from

HOLDING HOLLY

A Love and Football Novella

by Julie Brannagh

Holly Reynolds has a secret. Make that two. The first involves upholding her grandmother's hobby of answering Dear Santa letters from dozens of local schoolchildren. The second . . . well, he just came strolling in the door.

Derrick has never met a woman he wanted to bring home to meet his family, mostly because he keeps picking the wrong ones—until he runs into sweet, shy Holly Reynolds. Different from anyone he's ever known, Derrick realizes she might just be everything he needs.

"Do YOU NEED anything else right now?"

"I'm good," he said. "Then again, there's something I forgot."

"What do you need? Maybe I can help."

He moved closer to her, and she tipped her head back to look up at him. He reached out to cup one of her cheeks in his big hand. "I had a great time tonight. Thanks for having pizza with me."

"I had a nice time too. Th-thank you for inviting me," she stammered. There was so much more she'd like to say, but she was tongue-tied again. He was moving closer to her, and he reached out to put his drinking glass down on the counter.

"Maybe we could try this again when we're not in the middle of a snowstorm," he said. "I'd like a second date."

She started nodding like one of those bobbleheads, and forced herself to stop before he thought she was even more of a dork.

"Yes. I . . . Yes, I would too. I . . . that would be fun."

He took another half-step toward her. She did her best to pull in a breath.

"Normally, I would have kissed you good night at your

front door, but getting us inside before we froze to death seemed like the best thing to do right then," he said.

"Oh, yes. Absolutely. I—"

He reached out, slid his arms around her waist, and pulled her close. "I don't want to disrespect your grandma's wishes," he softly said. "She said I needed to treat you like a lady."

Holly almost let out a groan. She loved Grandma, but they needed to have a little chat later. "Sorry," she whispered.

He grinned at her. "I promise I'll behave myself, unless you don't want me to." She couldn't help it; she laughed. "Plus," he continued, "she said you have to be up very early in the morning to go to work, so we'll have to say good night."

Maybe she didn't need sleep. One thing's for sure, she had no interest in stepping away from him right now. He surrounded her, and she wanted to stay in his arms. Her heart was beating double-time, the blood was effervescent in her veins, and she summoned the nerve to move a little closer to him as she let out a happy sigh.

He kissed her cheek, and laid his scratchier one against hers. A few seconds later, she slid her arms around his neck too. "Good night, sweet Holly. Thanks for saving me from the snowstorm."

She had to laugh a little. "I think you saved *me*."

"We'll figure out who saved who later," he said. She felt his deep voice vibrating through her. She wished he'd kiss her again. Maybe she should kiss *him*.

He must have read her mind. He took her face in both

of his hands. "Don't tell your grandma," he whispered. His breath was warm on her cheek.

"Tell her what?"

"I'm going to kiss you."

Her head was bobbing around as she frantically nodded yes. She probably looked ridiculous, but he didn't seem to care. Her eyelids fluttered closed as his mouth touched hers, sweet and soft. It wasn't a long kiss, but she knew she'd never forget it. She felt the zing at his tender touch from the top of her head to her toes.

"A little more?" he asked.

"Oh, yes."

His arms wrapped around her again, and he slowly traced her lips with his tongue. It slid into her mouth. He tasted like the peppermints Noel Pizza kept in a jar on the front counter. They explored each other for a while as quietly as possible, but maybe not quietly enough.

"Holly, honey," her grandma called out from the family room. Holly was *absolutely* going to have a conversation with Grandma when Derrick was out of earshot, and she stifled a groan. All they were doing was a little kissing. He rested one big hand on her butt, which she enjoyed. "Would you please bring me some salad?"

Derrick let out a snort. "I'll get it for you, Miss Ruth," he said loudly enough for her grandma to hear.

"She's onto us," Holly said softly.

"Damn right." He grinned at her. "I'll see you tomorrow morning." His voice dropped. "We're *definitely* kissing on the second date."

"I'll look forward to that." She tried to pull in a breath.

Her head was spinning. She couldn't have stopped smiling if her life depended on it. "Are you sure you don't want to stay in my room instead? You need a good night's sleep. Don't you have to go to practice?"

"I'm sure your room is very comfortable, but I'll be fine out here. Sweet dreams," he said.

She felt him kiss the top of her head as he held her. She took a deep breath of his scent: clean skin, a whiff of expensive cologne, and freshly pressed clothes. "You, too," she whispered. She reached up to kiss his cheek. "Good night."

An Excerpt from

IT'S A WONDERFUL FIREMAN

A Bachelor Firemen Novella

by Jennifer Bernard

Hard-edged fireman Dean Mulligan has never been a big fan of Christmas. Twinkly lights and sparkly tinsel can't brighten the memories of too many years spent in ramshackle foster homes. When he's trapped in the burning wreckage of a holiday store, a Christmas angel arrives to open his eyes. But is it too late? This Christmas, it'll take an angel, a determined woman in love, and the entire Bachelor Firemen crew to make him believe . . . it is indeed a wonderful life.

HE'D FALLEN. MEMORY returned like water seeping into a basement. He'd been on the roof, and then he'd fallen through, and now he was . . . here. His PASS device was sounding in a high-decibel shriek, and its strobe light flashed, giving him quick, garish glimpses of his surroundings.

Mulligan looked around cautiously. The collapse must have put out much of the fire, because he saw only a few remnants of flames flickering listlessly on the far end of the space. Every surface was blackened and charred except for one corner, in which he spotted blurry flashes of gold and red and green.

He squinted and blinked his stinging eyes, trying to get them to focus. Finally the glimpse of gold formed itself into a display of dangling ball-shaped ornaments. He gawked at them. What were those things made from? How had they managed to survive the fire? He sought out the red and squinted at it through his face mask. A Santa suit, that's what it was, with great, blackened holes in the sleeves. It was propped on a rocking chair, which looked quite scorched. Mulligan wondered if a mannequin or something had been wearing the suit. If so, it was long gone. Next to the chair stood half of a plastic Christmas tree. One side had melted into black goo, while the other side looked pretty good.

Where am I? He formed the words with his mouth, though no sound came out. And it came back to him. Under the Mistletoe. He'd been about to die inside a Christmas store. But he hadn't. So far.

He tried to sit up, but something was pinning him down. Taking careful inventory, he realized that he lay on his left side, his tank pressing uncomfortably against his back, his left arm immobilized beneath him. What was on top of him? He craned his neck, feeling his face mask press against his chest. A tree. A freaking Christmas tree. Fully decorated and only slightly charred. It was enormous, at least ten feet high, its trunk a good foot in diameter. At its tip, an angel in a gold pleated skirt dangled precariously, as if she wanted to leap to the floor but couldn't summon the nerve. Steel brackets hung from the tree's trunk; it must have been mounted somewhere, maybe on a balcony or something. A few twisted ironwork bars confirmed that theory.

How the hell had a Christmas tree survived the inferno in here? It was wood! Granted, it was still a live tree, and its trunk and needles held plenty of sap. And fires were always unpredictable. The one thing you could be sure of was that they'd surprise you. Maybe the balcony had been protected somehow.

He moved his body, trying to shift the tree, but it was extremely heavy and he was pinned so flat he had no leverage. He spotted his radio a few feet away. It must have been knocked out of his pouch. Underneath the horrible, insistent whine of his PASS device, he heard the murmuring chatter of communication on the radio. If he could get a finger on it, he could hit his emergency trigger and switch to Channel 6, the May Day channel. His left arm was useless, but he could try with his right. But when he moved it, pain ripped through his shoulder.

Hell. Well, he could at least shut off the freaking PASS device. If a rapid intervention team made it in here, he'd yell for them. But no way could he stand listening to that sound for the next whatever-amount-of-time it took. Gritting his teeth against the agony, he reached for the device at the front of his turnout, then hit the button. The strobe light stopped and sudden silence descended, though his ears still rang. While he was at it, he checked the gauge that indicated how much air he had left in his tank. Ten minutes. He must have been in here for some time, sucking up air, since it was a thirty-minute tank.

A croak issued from his throat. "I'm in hell. No surprise."

Water. He needed water.

"I can't give you any water," a bright female voice said. For some reason, he had the impression that the angel on the tip of the Christmas tree had spoken. So he answered her back.

"Of course you can't. Because I'm in hell. They don't exactly hand out water bottles in hell."

"Who said you're in hell?"

Even though he watched the angel's lips closely, he didn't see them move. So it must not be her speaking. Besides, the voice seemed to be coming from behind him. "I figured it out all by myself."

Amazingly, he had no more trouble with his throat. Maybe he wasn't really speaking aloud. Maybe he was having this bizarre conversation with his own imagination. That theory was confirmed when a girl's shapely calves stepped into his field of vision. She wore red silk stockings the exact color of holly berries. She wore nothing else on her feet, which had a very familiar shape.

Lizzie.

His gaze traveled upward, along the swell of her calves. The stockings stopped just above her knees, where they were fastened by a red velvet bow. "Christmas stockings," he murmured.

"I told you."

"All right. I was wrong. Maybe it's heaven after all. Come here." He wanted to hold her close. His heart wanted to burst with joy that she was here with him, that he wasn't alone. That he wasn't going to die without seeing Lizzie again.

"I can't. There's a tree on top of you," she said in a teasing voice. "Either that, or you're very happy to see me."

"Oh, you noticed that? You can move it, can't you? Either you're an angel and have magical powers, or you're real and you can push it off me."

She laughed. A real Lizzie laugh, starting as a giggle and swooping up the register until it became a whoop. "Do you really think an angel would dress like this?"

"Hmm, good point. What are you wearing besides those stockings? I can't even see. At least step closer so I can see."

"Fine." A blur of holly red, and then she perched on

the pile of beams and concrete that blocked the east end of his world. In addition to the red stockings, she wore a red velvet teddy and a green peaked hat, which sat at an angle on her flowing dark hair. Talk about a "hot elf" look.

"Whoa. How'd you do that?"

"You did it."

"I did it?" How could he do it? He was incapacitated. Couldn't even move a finger. Well, maybe he could move a finger. He gave it a shot, wiggling the fingers on both hands. At least he wasn't paralyzed.

But he did seem to be mentally unstable. "I'm hallucinating, aren't I?"

"Bingo."

An Excerpt from

ONCE UPON A HIGHLAND CHRISTMAS

by Lecia Cornwall

Lady Alanna McNabb is bound by duty to her family, who insist she must marry a gentleman of wealth and title. When she meets the man of her dreams, she knows it's much too late, but her heart is no longer hers.

Laird Iain MacGillivray is on his way to propose to another woman when he discovers Alanna half-frozen in the snow and barely alive. She isn't his to love, yet she's everything he's ever wanted.

As Christmas comes closer, the snow thickens, and the magic grows stronger. Alanna and Iain must choose between desire and duty, love and obligation.

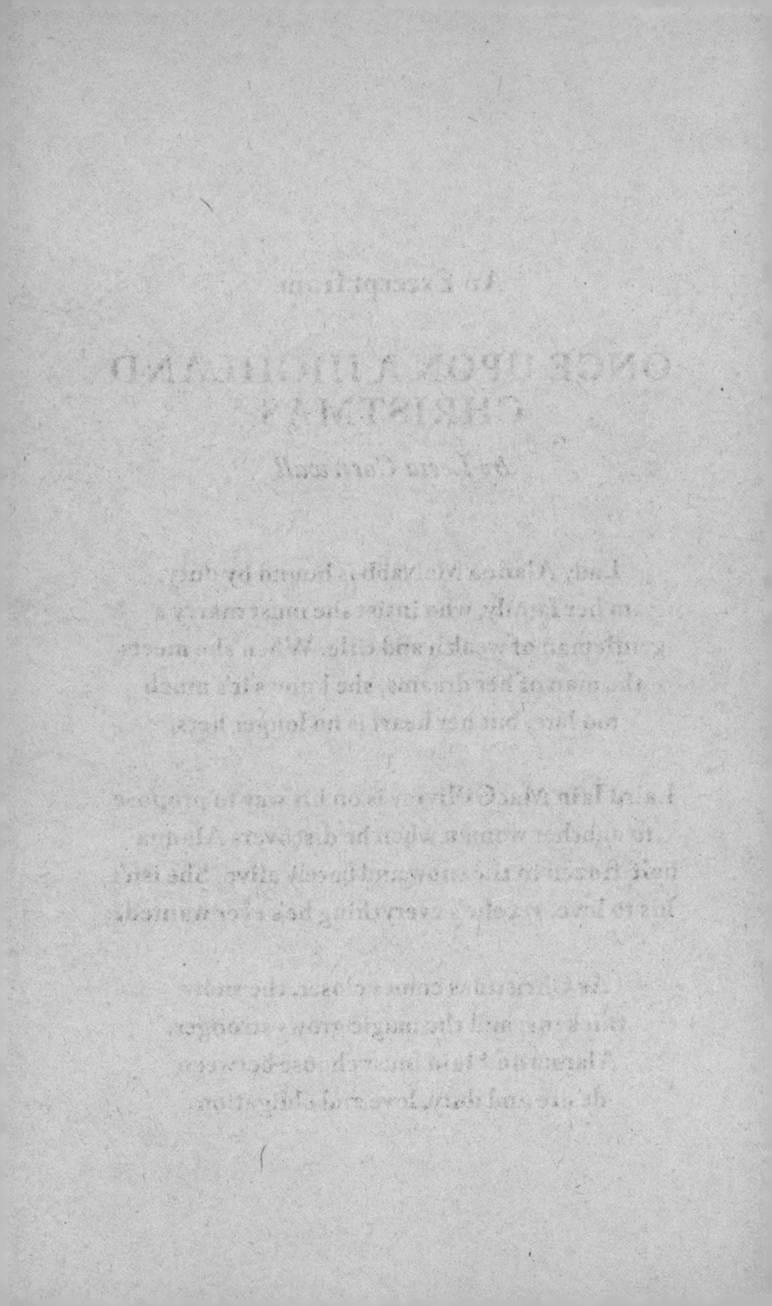

Alanna McNabb woke with a terrible headache. In fact, every inch of her body ached. She could smell peat smoke, and dampness, and hear wind. She remembered the storm and opened her eyes. She was in a small dark room, a hut, she realized, a shieling, perhaps, or was it one of the crofter's cottages at Glenlorne? Was she home, among the people who knew her, loved her? She looked around, trying to decide where exactly she was, whose home she was in. The roof beams above her head were blackened with age and soot, and a thick stoneware jug dangled from a nail hammered into the beam as a hook. But that offered no clues at all—it was the same in every Highland cott. She turned her head a little, knowing there would be a hearth, and—

A few feet from her, a man crouched by the fire.

A very big, very naked man.

She stared at his back, which was broad and smooth. She took note of well-muscled arms as he poked the fire. She followed the bumps of his spine down to a pair of dimples just above his round white buttocks.

Her throat dried. She tried to sit up, but pain shot through her body, and the room wavered before her eyes. Her leg was on fire, pure agony. She let out a soft cry.

He half turned at the sound and glanced over his shoulder, and she had a quick impression of a high cheekbone lit by the firelight, and a gleaming eye that instantly widened with surprise. He dropped the poker and fell on his backside with a grunt.

"You're awake!" he cried. She stared at him sprawled on the hearthstones, and he gasped again and cupped his hands over his— She shut her eyes tight, as he grabbed the nearest thing at hand to cover himself—a corner of the plaid—but she yanked it back, holding tight. He instantly let go and reached for the closest garment dangling from the line above him, which turned out to be her red cloak. He wrapped it awkwardly around his waist, trying to rise to his feet at the same time. He stood above her in his makeshift kilt, holding it in place with a white knuckled grip, his face almost as red as the wool. She kept her eyes on his face and pulled her own blanket tight around her throat.

"I see you're awake," he said, staring at her, his voice an octave lower now. "How do you feel?"

How *did* she feel? She assessed her injuries, tried to remember the details of how she came to be here, wherever here might be. She recalled being lost in a storm, and falling. There'd been blood on her glove. She frowned. After that she didn't remember anything at all.

She shifted carefully, and the room dissolved. She saw stars, and black spots, and excruciating pain streaked through her body, radiating from her knee. She gasped, panted, stiffened against it.

"Don't move," he said, holding out a hand, fingers splayed, though he didn't touch her. He grinned, a sudden flash of white teeth, the firelight bright in his eyes. "I found you out in the snow. I feared . . . well, it doesn't matter now. Your knee is injured, cut, and probably sprained, but it isn't broken," he said in a rush. He grinned again, as if that was all very good news, and dropped to one knee beside her. "You've got some color back."

He reached out and touched her cheek with the back of his hand, a gentle enough caress, but she flinched away and gasped at the pain that caused. He dropped his hand at once, looked apologetic. "I mean no harm, lass—I was just checking that you're warm, but not too warm. Or too cold . . ." He was babbling, and he broke off, gave her a wan smile, and stood up again, holding onto her cloak, taking a step back away from her. Was he blushing, or was it the light of the fire on his skin? She tried not to stare at the breadth of his naked chest, or the naked legs that showed beneath the trailing edge of the cloak.

She gingerly reached down under the covers and found her knee was bound up in a bandage of some sort. He turned away, flushing again, and she realized the plaid had slipped down. She was as naked as he was. She gasped, drew the blanket tight to her chin, and stared at him. She looked up and saw that her clothes were hanging on a line above the fireplace—all of them, even her shift.

"Where—?" she swallowed. Her voice was hoarse, her throat as raw as her knee. "Who are you?" she tried again. She felt hot blood fill her cheeks, and panic formed a tight knot in her chest, and she tried again to remember what had happened, but her mind was blank. If he was—unclothed, and she was equally unclothed—

"What—" she began again, then swallowed the question she couldn't frame. She hardly knew what to ask first, Where, Who, or What? Her mind was moving slowly, her thoughts as thick and rusty as her tongue.

"You're safe, lass," he said, and she wondered if she was. She stared at him. She'd seen men working in the summer sun, their shirts off, their bodies tanned, their muscles straining, but she'd never thought anything of it. This—he—was different. And she was as naked as he was.

An Excerpt from

RUNNING HOT

A Bad Boys Undercover Novella

by HelenKay Dimon

Ward Bennett and Tasha Gregory aren't on the same team. But while hunting a dictator on the run, these two must decide whether they can trust one another—and their ability to stay professional. Working together might just make everyone safer, but getting cozy . . . might just get them killed.

"Take your clothes off."

He looked at her as if she'd lost her mind. "Excuse me?"

"You're attracted to me." Good Lord, now Tasha was waving her hands in the air. Once she realized it, she stopped. Curled her hands into balls at her sides. "I find you . . . fine."

Ward covered his mouth and produced a fake cough. She assumed it hid a smile. That was almost enough to make her rescind the offer.

"Really? That's all you can muster?" This time he did smile. "You think I'm fine?"

He was hot and tall and had a face that played in her head long after she closed her eyes each night. And that body. Long and lean, with the stalk of a predator. Ward was a man who protected and fought. She got the impression he wrestled demons that had to do with reconciling chivalry and decency with the work they performed.

The combination of all that made her wild with need. "Your clothes are still on."

"Are you saying you want to—"

Since he was saying the sentence so slowly—emphasizing, and halting after, each word—she finished it fast. "Shag."

Both eyebrows rose now. "Please tell me that's British for 'have sex.' "

"Yes."

He blew out a long, staggered breath. "Thank God, because right now my body is in a race to see what will explode first, my brain or my dick."

Uh? "Is that a compliment?"

"Believe it or not, yes." Two steps, and he was in front of her, his fingers playing with the small white button at the top of her slim tee. "So, are you talking about now or sometime in the future to celebrate ending Tigana?"

Both. "I need to work off this extra energy and get back in control." She was half-ready to rip off her clothes and throw him on the mattress.

Maybe he knew because he just stood there and stared at her, his gaze not leaving her face.

She stared back.

Just as he started to lower his head, a ripple moved through her. She shoved a hand against his shoulder. "Don't think that I always break protocol like this."

"I don't care if you do." He ripped his shirt out of his pants and whipped it over his head, revealing miles of tanned muscles and skin.

"You're taking off your clothes." Not the smartest thing she'd ever said, but it was out there and she couldn't snatch it back.

"You're the boss, remember?"

A shot of regret nearly knocked her over. Not at making the pass but at wanting him this much in the first place.

Here and now, when her mind should be on the assignment, not on his chest.

She'd buried this part of herself for so long under a pile of work and professionalism that bringing it out now made her twitchy. "This isn't—"

His hands went to her arms, and he brushed those palms up and down, soothing her. "Do you want me?"

She couldn't lie. He had to feel it in the tremor shaking through her. "Yes."

"Then stop justifying not working this very second and enjoy. It won't make you less of a professional."

That was exactly what she needed to hear. "Okay."

His hands stopped at her elbows, and he dragged her in closer, until the heat of his body radiated against her. "You're a stunning woman, and we've been circling each other for days. Honestly, your ability to handle weapons only makes you hotter in my eyes."

The words spun through her. They felt so good. So right. "Not the way I would say it, but okay."

"You want me. I sure as hell want you. We need to lie low until it gets dark and we can hide our movements better." The corner of his mouth kicked up in a smile filled with promise. "And, for the record, there is nothing sexier than a woman who goes after what she wants."

He meant it. She knew it with every cell inside her.

Screw being safe.

Here and now, when her mind should be on the assignment, not on his chest.

She'd hoped this part of herself was long gone, or a pile of stock and professionalism that bringing it out now made her twitchy. "This isn't—"

His hands went to her arms, and he brushed them, palms up and down, soothing her. "Do you want me?"

She couldn't lie. He had to feel it in the tremor shooting through her. "Yes."

"Then stop worrying, not working this very second and enjoy. It won't make you less of a professional."

That was exactly what she needed to hear. "Okay."

He gently gripped her elbows, and then tugged her in closer, until the heat of his body radiated against her. "You're a stunning woman, and we've been circling each other for days. Honestly, your ability to handle weapons only makes you hotter in my eyes."

The words spun through her. They felt so good, also right. "Not the way I would say it, but okay."

"You want me. I sure as hell want you. We need to lie low until it gets dark and we can hide our movements better." The [illegible] of his mouth [illegible], a [illegible] filled with promise. "And, for the record, there is nothing sexier than a woman who goes after what she wants."

He meant it. She knew it with [illegible] will make her [illegible] being safe.

An Excerpt from

SINFUL REWARDS 1

A Billionaires and Bikers Novella

by Cynthia Sax

Belinda "Bee" Carter is a good girl; at least, that's what she tells herself. And a good girl deserves a nice guy—just like the gorgeous and moody billionaire Nicolas Rainer. Or so she thinks, until she takes a look through her telescope and sees a naked, tattooed man on the balcony across the courtyard. He has been watching her, and that makes him all the more enticing. But when a mysterious and anonymous text message dares her to do something bad, she must decide if she is really the good girl she has always claimed to be, or if she's willing to risk everything for her secret fantasy of being watched.

An Avon Red Novella

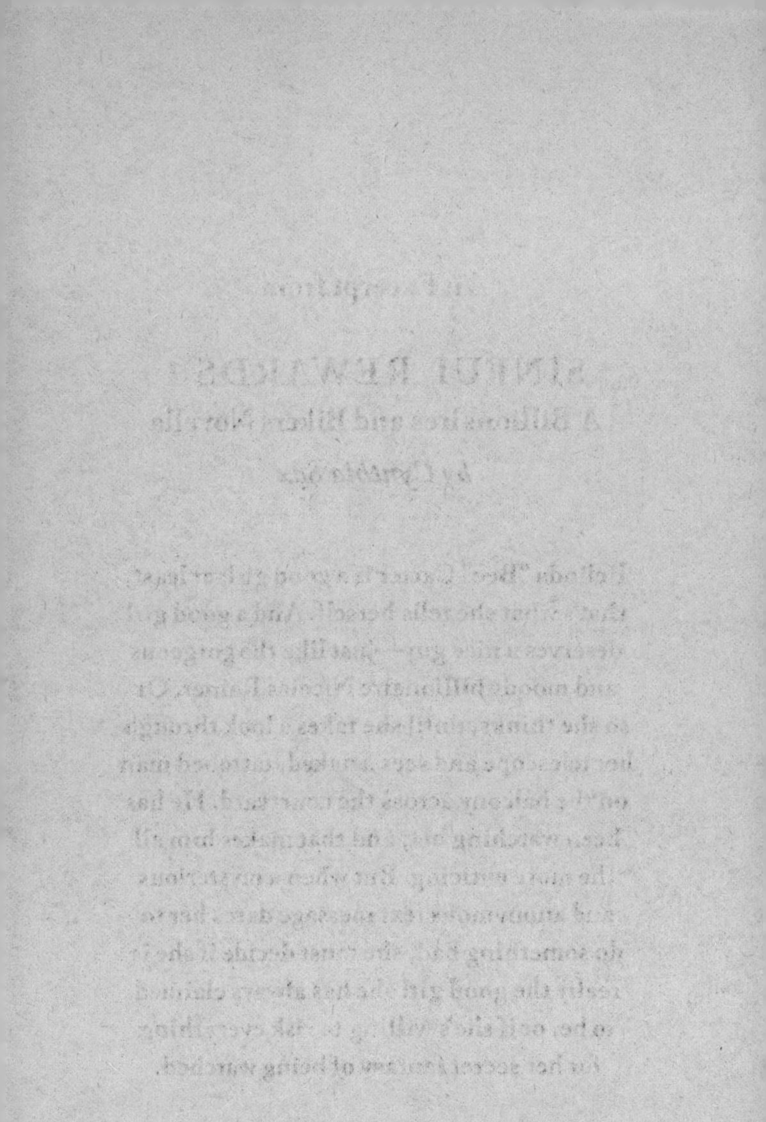

I'd told Cyndi I'd never use it, that it was an instrument purchased by perverts to spy on their neighbors. She'd laughed and called me a prude, not knowing that I was one of those perverts, that I secretly yearned to watch and be watched, to care and be cared for.

If I'm cautious, and I'm always cautious, she'll never realize I used her telescope this morning. I swing the tube toward the bench and adjust the knob, bringing the mysterious object into focus.

It's a phone. Nicolas's phone. I bounce on the balls of my feet. This is a sign, another declaration from fate that we belong together. I'll return Nicolas's much-needed device to him. As a thank you, he'll invite me to dinner. We'll talk. He'll realize how perfect I am for him, fall in love with me, marry me.

Cyndi will find a fiancé also—everyone loves her—and we'll have a double wedding, as sisters of the heart often do. It'll be the first wedding my family has had in generations.

Everyone will watch us as we walk down the aisle. I'll wear a strapless white Vera Wang mermaid gown with organza and lace details, crystal and pearl embroidery accents, the bodice fitted, and the skirt hemmed for my shorter height. My hair will be swept up. My shoes—

Voices murmur outside the condo's door, the sound piercing my delightful daydream. I swing the telescope upward, not wanting to be caught using it. The snippets of conversation drift away.

I don't relax. If the telescope isn't positioned in the same way as it was last night, Cyndi will realize I've been using it. She'll tease me about being a fellow pervert, sharing the story, embellished for dramatic effect, with her stern, serious dad—or, worse, with Angel, that snobby friend of hers.

I'll die. It'll be worse than being the butt of jokes in high school because that ridicule was about my clothes and this will center on the part of my soul I've always kept hidden. It'll also be the truth, and I won't be able to deny it. I am a pervert.

I have to return the telescope to its original position. This is the only acceptable solution. I tap the metal tube.

Last night, my man-crazy roommate was giggling over the new guy in three-eleven north. The previous occupant was a gray-haired, bowtie-wearing tax auditor, his luxurious accommodations supplied by Nicolas. The most exciting thing he ever did was drink his tea on the balcony.

According to Cyndi, the new occupant is a delicious piece of man candy—tattooed, buff, and head-to-toe lickable. He was completing armcurls outside, and she enthusiastically counted his reps, oohing and aahing over his bulging biceps, calling to me to take a look.

I resisted that temptation, focusing on making macaroni and cheese for the two of us, the recipe snagged from the diner my mom works in. After we scarfed down dinner, Cyndi licking her plate clean, she left for the club and hasn't returned.

Three-eleven north is the mirror condo to ours. I straighten the telescope. That position looks about right, but then, the imitation UGGs I bought in my second year of college looked about right also. The first time I wore the boots in the rain, the sheepskin fell apart, leaving me barefoot in Economics 201.

Unwilling to risk Cyndi's friendship on "about right," I gaze through the eyepiece. The view consists of rippling golden planes, almost like . . .

Tanned skin pulled over defined abs.

I blink. It can't be. I take another look. A perfect pearl of perspiration clings to a puckered scar. The drop elongates more and more, stretching, snapping. It trickles downward, navigating the swells and valleys of a man's honed torso.

No. I straighten. This is wrong. I shouldn't watch our sexy neighbor as he stands on his balcony. If anyone catches me . . .

Parts 1 – 6 available now!

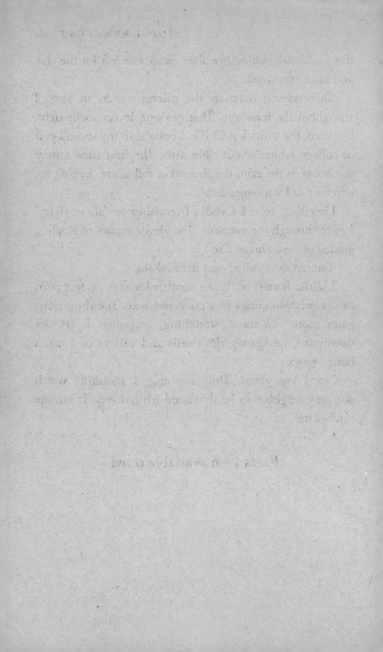

An Excerpt from

RETURN TO CLAN SINCLAIR

A Clan Sinclair Novella

by Karen Ranney

When Ceana Sinclair Mead married the youngest son of an Irish duke, she never dreamed that seven years later her beloved Peter would die. Her three brothers-in-law think she should be grateful to remain a proper widow. After three years of this, she's ready to scream. She escapes to Scotland, only to discover she's so much more than just the Widow Mead.

In Scotland, Ceana crosses paths with Bruce Preston, an American tasked with a dangerous mission by her brother, Macrath. Bruce is too attractive for her peace of mind, but she still finds him fascinating. Their one night together is more wonderful than Ceana could have imagined, and she has never felt more alive.

The darkness was nearly absolute, leaving her no choice but to stretch her hands out on either side of her, fingertips brushing against the stone walls. The incline was steep, further necessitating she take her time. Yet at the back of her mind was the last image she had of Carlton, his bright impish grin turning to horror as he glanced down.

The passage abruptly ended in a mushroom-shaped cavern. This was the grotto she'd heard so much about, with its flue in the middle and its broad, wide window looking out over the beach and the sea. She raced to the window, hopped up on the sill nature had created over thousands of years and leaned out.

A naked man reached up, grabbed Carlton as he fell. After he lowered the boy to the sand, he turned and smiled at her.

Carlton was racing across the beach, glancing back once or twice to see if he was indeed free. The rope made of sheets was hanging limply from his window.

The naked man was standing there with hands on his hips, staring at her in full frontal glory.

She hadn't seen many naked men, the last being her husband. The image in front of her now was so startling she couldn't help but stare. A smile was dawning on the stranger's full lips, one matched by his intent brown eyes. No, not quite brown, were they? They were like the finest Scottish whiskey touched with sunlight.

Her gaze danced down his strong and corded neck to broad shoulders etched with muscle. His chest was broad and muscled as well, tapering down to a slim waist and hips.

Even semiflaccid, his manhood was quite impressive.

The longer she watched, the more impressive it became.

What on earth was a naked man doing on Macrath's beach?

To her utter chagrin, the stranger turned and presented his backside to her, glancing over his shoulder to see if she approved of the sight.

She withdrew from the window, cheeks flaming. What on earth had she been doing? Who was she to gawk at a naked man as if she'd never before seen one?

Now that she knew Carlton was going to survive his escape, she should retreat immediately to the library.

"You'd better tell Alistair his brother's gotten loose again. Are you the new governess?"

She turned to find him standing in the doorway, still naked.

She pressed her fingers against the base of her throat and counseled herself to appear unaffected.

"I warn you, the imp escapes at any chance. You'll have your hands full there."

The look of fright on Carlton's face hadn't been fear of the distance to the beach, but the fact that he'd been caught.

She couldn't quite place the man's accent, but it wasn't Scottish. American, perhaps. What did she care where he came from? The problem was what he was doing here.

"I'm not a governess," she said. "I'm Macrath's sister, Ceana."

He bent and retrieved his shirt from a pile of clothes beside the door, taking his time with it. Shouldn't he have begun with his trousers instead?

"Who are you?" she asked, looking away as he began to don the rest of his clothing.

She'd had two children. She was well versed in matters of nature. She knew quite well what a man's body looked like. The fact that his struck her as singularly attractive was no doubt due to the fact she'd been a widow for three years.

"Well, Ceana Sinclair, is it all that important you know who I am?"

"It isn't Sinclair," she said. "It's Mead."

He tilted his head and studied her.

"Is Mr. Mead visiting along with you?"

She stared down at her dress of unremitting black. "I'm a widow," she said.

A shadow flitted over his face "Are you? Did Macrath know you were coming?"

"No," she said. "Does it matter? He's my brother. He's family. And why would you be wanting to know?"

He shrugged, finished buttoning his pants and began to don his shoes.

"Who are you?" she asked again.

"I'm a detective," he said. "My company was hired by your brother."

"Why?"

"Now that's something I'm most assuredly not going to tell you," he said. "It was nice meeting you, Mrs. Mead. I hope to see more of you before I leave."

And she hoped to see much, much less of him.

An Excerpt from

RETURN OF THE BAD GIRL

by Codi Gary

When Caroline Willis learns that her perfect apartment has been double-booked—to a dangerously hot bad boy—her bad-girl reputation comes out in full force. But as close quarters begin to ignite the sizzling chemistry between them, she's left wondering: Bad boy plus bad girl equals nothing but trouble . . . right?

"I FEEL LIKE you keep looking for something more to me, but what you know about me is it. There's no 'deep down,' no mistaking my true character. I am bad news." He waited, listening for the tap of her retreating feet or the slam of the door, but only silence met his ears, then the soft sound of shoes on the cement floor—getting closer to him instead of farther away.

Fingers trailed feather-light touches over his lower back. "This scar on your back—is that from the accident?"

Her caress made his skin tingle as he shook his head. "I was knocked down by one of my mother's boyfriends and landed on a glass table."

"What about here?" Her hand had moved onto his right shoulder.

"It was a tattoo I had removed. In prison, you're safer if you belong, so—"

"I understand," she said, cutting him off. Had she heard the pain in his voice, or did she really understand?

He turned around before she could point out any more scars. "What are you doing?"

She looked him in the eye and touched the side of his neck, where his tattoo began, spreading all the way down past his shoulder and over his chest. "You say you're damaged. That you're bad news and won't ever change."

"Yeah?"

To his surprise, she dropped her hand to his and brought it up to her collarbone, where his finger felt a rough, puckered line.

"This is a knife wound—just a scratch, really—that I got from a man who used to come see me dance at the strip club. He was constantly asking me out, and I always let him down easy. But one night, after I'd had a shitty day, I told him I would never go out with an old, ugly fuck like him. He was waiting by my car when I got off work."

His rage blazed at this phantom from her past. "What happened?"

"I pulled a move I'd learned from one of the bouncers. Even though he still cut me, I was able to pick up a handful of gravel and throw it in his face. I made it to the front door of the club, and he took off. They arrested him on assault charges, and it turned out he had an outstanding warrant. I never saw him again."

Caroline pulled him closer, lifting her arm for him to see a jagged scar along her forearm. "This is from a broken beer bottle I got sliced with when a woman came into my bar in San Antonio, looking for her husband. She didn't take it well when she found out he had a girlfriend on the side, and when I stepped in to stop her from attacking him, she sliced me."

He couldn't stop his hand from sliding up over her soft skin until it rested on the back of her neck, his fingers pressing into her flesh until she tilted her chin up to meet his gaze.

"What's your point with all the show-and-tell, Caroline?"

She reached out and smoothed his chest with her hand. "I don't care how damaged you are, because I am just as broken, maybe more so."

Her words tore at him, twisting him up inside as his other hand cupped the back of her head. "You don't want to go here with me, princess. I'm only going to break your heart."

The laugh that passed those beautiful lips was bitter and sad. "Trust me, my heart was shattered long before I ever met you."

Gabe wanted her, wanted to believe that he could find comfort in her body without the complications that would inevitably come, but he'd seen her heart firsthand. She had one. It might be wrapped up in a mile-thick layer of cowhide, but a part of Caroline Willis was still open to new emotions. New love.

And he wasn't.

But he wanted to kiss her anyway.

He dropped his head until his lips hovered above hers, and he watched as they parted when he came closer. Her hot breath teased his mouth, and he couldn't stop while she was warm and willing. He might not get another chance to taste her, and while a better man would have walked away, he wasn't that guy.